DON'T KNOW A GOOD THING

DON'T KNOW A GOOD THING

The Asham Award Short-Story Collection

Edited by Kate Pullinger

BLOOMSBURY

First published 2006

Selection copyright © 2006 by The Asham Trust
Foreword copyright © 2006 by Carole Buchan

The copyright of the individual stories remains with the respective authors

The moral right of the authors has been asserted

Bloomsbury Publishing Plc, 36 Soho Square, London W1D 3QY

A CIP catalogue record for this book is available from the British Library

ISBN 0 7475 8183 5
9780747581833

10 9 8 7 6 5 4 3 2 1

Typeset by Hewer Text UK Ltd, Edinburgh
Printed in Great Britain by Clays Ltd, St Ives plc

All papers used by Bloomsbury Publishing are natural,
recyclable products made from wood grown in well-managed
forests. The manufacturing processes conform to the environmental
regulations of the country of origin

www.bloomsbury.com/asham

www.ashamaward.com

CONTENTS

THE ASHAM AWARD 2005

First prize   *The Wing* by Annie Kirby

Second prize   *Hwang* by Carys Davies

Third prize   *Holding the Baby* by Francesca Kay

Winner of the Asham Bursary, sponsored by the Arts
Council of England: Lianne Kolirin for *Elvis Has Entered
the Building*

*The Asham Literary Endowment Trust wishes to thank
the judges of this year's Asham Award:*

Lynne Truss, Louise Doughty and Chris Meade

*and the commissioned writers who have contributed to
this collection:*

Trezza Azzopardi, Louise Doughty, Helen Dunmore, Helen
Simpson, Lynne Truss and Marina Warner.

CAROLE BUCHAN

Foreword

I T was ten years ago that the first Asham Award for new women writers was launched in Sussex. Named after the house where Virginia Woolf once lived, the award was set up to provide a vehicle for the new writers of tomorrow.

Few could have guessed then that within a decade the Asham Literary Endowment Trust, which administers the award, would be in the forefront of the successful campaign to raise the status of the short story in contemporary literature and to give fiction a fresh new look. These days mainstream publishers are producing anthologies of short fiction by both new and established writers. The work of many of the great short story writers of the past is being re-examined and re-evaluated and the genre is no longer seen merely as the answer to the pressures of twenty-first century living, but is valued as an art form in its own right.

Alongside this commitment to the short story is the Asham Trust's commitment to the writers themselves, both new and established. The past ten years of the Asham Award have seen some of the most exciting and innovative new fiction from women across the British Isles. Many have gone on to carve out new careers as writers, journalists and critics. Erica Wagner, for example, was one of the winners of the first award with her story *Pyramid*. She was already literary editor of *The Times*, but has since published a range of fiction and biography and has judged some of the foremost literary prizes, including the Man Booker, Whitbread, Forward and Orange.

Linda Leatherbarrow's story *Lost Boys* was published by Serpent's Tail in the third anthology. She has won a number of literary prizes, and recently had a collection of short stories – *Essential Kit* – published by the Maia Press. In addition, her inspirational teaching on the creative writing MA at Middlesex University has produced a number of Asham prizewinners, including Victoria Briggs, who won first prize in 2003, was signed up by an agent and is now working part time in order to concentrate on her writing. Other successful students include Hilary Plews (who won third prize in 2003), Lianne Kolirin (who won this year's Asham Bursary) and Jessica Bowman, author of the title story in this collection.

Ann Jolly won first prize in 2000 with her story *Girls in their Loveliness*. Since then she has been Writer in Residence at Dartmoor Prison and has produced a book and CD of the prisoners' work and has helped them to start their own magazine.

Rachael McGill has developed a career in the theatre. A winner in 2003, her plays deal with social issues such as new variant CJD and race politics in London. But her first love will always be prose writing. Awards like Asham, she says, are not only important for the encouragement they give writers, but also for valuing the form of the short story.

The winner of this year's first prize – Annie Kirby – is trying to put together a collection of short stories. She is also working on a novel, called *Blood Hands Moon Snow*, which she describes as 'a big melodramatic generation-spanning story of selkies, Gothic novelists and transvestite fishermen!'.

The Asham Trust has a policy of linking new and established writers through its anthology, its mentoring schemes with young people and its workshop programme. We are immensely grateful to those writers who have supported our work over the years and who have generously given their time to those setting out on their careers. Special thanks should go to our editor Kate Pullinger and to Lynne Truss, Louise Doughty and Helen Dunmore – each of whom has been involved with Asham from the beginning. Our thanks also to Serpent's Tail, who supported us when we were a totally unknown organisation, and to Bloomsbury, who have successfully taken the Asham Award into the next decade.

As Stephen Vincent Benet said, 'A short story is something that can be read in an hour and remembered for a lifetime.' We hope you will find stories in this collection which will do just that.

Carole Buchan,
Administrator, Asham Literary Endowment Trust,
Lewes, East Sussex.

- *If you love short stories, look out for the short-story festival – Small Wonder – organised jointly by the Asham and Charleston Trusts to be held at Charleston, near Lewes, in September 2006.*
- *For more information visit www.ashamaward.com or www.charleston.org.uk from July 2006.*

SALLY HINCHCLIFFE

In Heaven There Is No Beer

THE MAN seemed to know only the one song, a drinking song. He sang it as she might sing ordinary songs, pop songs: under his breath, whistling, trying out different keys and tempos, different effects. He was a thin, ordinary man with a failed drooping moustache and he walked around the garden – yard – in his vest, singing. *In heaven there is no beer*. He sang it slowly, a funereal dirge. Whistled it in a minor key with flourishes. He even sang it in the evening, sitting out on the porch, drinking beer among the moths that danced around his head.

Lucy could see him from her own, or rather, her borrowed, porch. Hers was boxed in, netted. *West Nile Virus has been reported here*, her invisible hosts had written, *so don't sit out without protection. We don't want to alarm you but West Nile Virus can Kill!* She reflected that she was a long way west of the Nile here, but dutifully wore long sleeves and burned a citronella candle on the porch. And listened to her borrowed neighbour singing to the moths and mosquitoes in his sleeveless vest.

The little boy sang the song too, in his piping voice. In heaven, there is no beer. He ran around the garden alone, sat and dug in the flowerbeds, and sang to himself, rocking. How old? Three? Four? There seemed to be only the man and the kid. The house was enclosed by a chain link fence and the kid tore around inside its boundaries. He seemed clean enough, safe, well fed. The neighbour didn't seem to be the kind of man who would bathe a kid, feed it, change it. She wondered if there was a mother somewhere, or a grandmother.

Her hosts had left no notes about their neighbour. She wondered what they were making of her own neighbours, in London. From the friendly tone of their notes she could imagine them introducing themselves, even inviting themselves into the mirror image houses that flanked hers; houses that she had never visited. She had left no notes, only a map. She liked maps and she'd taken care in drawing them one. The tube station. The bus stop drawn in with little double-decker buses, Tescos, the fishmonger she never had time to visit.

Rainbow foods is the nearest big grocery store. West on I94 junction with County road H. Right at the stop lights and you can't miss it. She set out in her borrowed car and missed it. Drove at random down highways that seemed large enough to land aeroplanes on. The sides of the roads were scattered with little orange flags, and prairie flowers. She drove the swooping curves of an intersection but it didn't intersect with County road H. She bought milk and cookies at a gas station and navigated herself back by following the town's water tower. Tomorrow she'd shop near the library, try and buy a road map.

As she got out of the car she saw her neighbour getting out of his, carrying brown paper bags marked Rainbow.

'Did you just come from the supermarket?'

In London she'd have got a sarcastic answer, but this was the Midwest. He gave her the sort of instructions she needed, turn left, third right, 'bout half a mile. He didn't comment on her accent, her sudden appearance in his neighbour's house. She smiled at the kid, who hid his face, then peeped out and smiled back at her with such sweetness that her heart turned over. As she backed out of the drive again, she saw the child pick up one bag almost as large as he was and she found she couldn't finally pull away until she had watched him safely negotiate the steps one at a time and disappear into the dark interior of the house.

The house hummed with strange appliances that squatted in the basement. Garbage disposal. Furnace. The washing machine swallowed a whole week's worth of laundry and left room for more. There was an elaborate system for watering the lawn. *Turn on Sprinkler A on Monday, B on Wednesday, A on Friday, and run them both at the weekend. The Parker kid will come and mow Tuesdays.* Her garden had no fence and only the subtle differences in grass heights marked the transition between her house and the neighbours on the left. The Parker kid must mow them on different days. Beyond the chain link on the right the grass was brown and patchy and nobody seemed to mow it much. The boy dug in the bare earth and the prairie flowers she'd seen on the highway bloomed between neglected shrubs. She knew them, grew Rudbeckia and Goldenrod in her own garden at home. She wondered if her invisible hosts, staring out of her kitchen window with her coffee mugs in their hands, thought she was letting it go to weeds.

During the week she ran the sprinklers in the evening, when she had come back from the library. She couldn't bear to run them all day. On the Friday she sat on her porch with her citronella candle and listened to the shushing noise of sprinkler A as it traversed the grass, and the flat *splat splat splat* as it crossed the paving of the driveway. The evenings had been mostly hot and humid and she was grateful for the little breeze that occasionally lifted the pages of her book, bringing with it a snatch of song. He was in a good mood tonight with his beer, she thought, and he sang his ditty cheerfully. In heaven there is no beer. It almost amounted to a philosophy, or maybe a religion.

The library closed early on Saturdays and didn't open at all on Sundays. The first weekend a friend of a colleague, the one who'd arranged her research visit and sorted out her temporary reader's card, had taken her out to his lake house with his family. This weekend, though, he was away and after she had set the sprinklers and navigated her way to and around the grocery store she had almost two whole days left of her own company. *Mrs Diaz comes and cleans Thursdays. Leave any ironing in the laundry room.* She realised how much of her English life was spent simply doing the things that her invisible hosts' invisible army did on named days of the week. Mrs Diaz had left a trail of vacuuming marks on the thick carpets which Lucy's small comings and goings had done little to disturb. A pile of her folded clothes still formed a neat squared pillar on the dresser.

Wandering out on to the thick grass, dodging the rainbow spray, she heard a treble voice singing. The kid was watching her. In heaven there is no beer. He sang it with real longing. He was wearing only a pair of shorts and his dirty bare feet clutched the damp edges of the mud where the sprinklers invaded through the fence. The air stood motionless under the shade trees.

'You want to go play in the sprinklers?'

He nodded.

'Come on then'

But the gate was locked.

'Where's your dad?'

He looked blank.

She reached over and picked him up. He was a solid weight in her arms but she could lift him over the fence.

'We'll put you back when you've cooled off, hey?'

The kid had an action figure in one hand, and he and it danced in the spray, the kid stolid, serious. The action figure betrayed no emotion beyond a frozen snarl. Its hands reached into empty air.

'What's your name?'

'Tyler.'

'I'm Lucy.'

The kid nodded. She sat on the front step and watched him. When he'd had enough he rolled on the thick grass and laughed. He came up speckled with cut green ends. She danced decorously through the sprinkler, pretending to avoid its swinging arc, and clutched her skirts when it caught her. He gurgled with laughter and held his hand over the jet, holding it and releasing it so it caught her full in the face. She didn't see the neighbour's low brown car as it turned the corner. 'Hey, miss!'

Caught, she stopped laughing suddenly. So did Tyler. They both stood frozen and guilty.

'He get out of the yard himself?'

She shook her head, felt herself blushing.

'He just seemed so hot. I'm sorry.'

'Yeah.' It was a neutral sound, neither angry nor mollified.

'You shouldn't leave him on his own like that.'

He stared at her. The kid looked back and forth between them as though he was used to watching fights. His lip wobbled. The man squatted before him, ruffled his hair fiercely.

Terse? Is it a lie?
we don't know.
Expantion → relaying information.
Description.

leaning
tip
at
crate
experts
putting up a
front

'I only left you for a few minutes, ain't that right?' He rose and turned on his heel and went into the house. Tyler trotted in after him. He still had her grass sticking to his shoulder blades but he didn't turn once and look back.

The weather remained hot and still into the evening. Lucy gathered up her peace offering, the beer cold in her hand. The neighbour had left off his porch light but she could see the periodic glow of his cigarette as he drew on it, and heard the light crack of a can opening.

She put one hand on the fence and listened as he sang into the dark. He stopped singing after a while and the glow of the cigarette turned towards her expectantly.

'I'm sorry,' she said. 'It was none of my business.'

He waited a long time before answering. 'You were right. But I have no choice, sometimes.' There was a pause. She could hear the throbbing of strange insects. 'Gate's open.'

'I'll get my citronella candle. West Nile Virus can Kill.'

The beer was thin on her tongue, but the cold was welcome. The backs of her thighs prickled against the vinyl of the porch seat.

'You a friend of the Kiesers?'

'Who? Oh, no. We swapped houses, that's all.' She had thought it would be weird inhabiting another person's life, living in their house. She hadn't expected to take on another person's neighbour as well. She realised she was hungry for conversation, had been living with her own thoughts buzzing round her head for too long. She was halfway through her research and she had spoken to almost no one for a week.

'So they living in yours?'

'Yes. I wonder if they like it.'

He just smiled, gave a brief exhaling laugh. Lucy wondered at the private joke, but he didn't elaborate, and she didn't ask.

'Reckon they're sitting on your porch right now?'

'Or my neighbour's.'

'Makes you think.' Of what, she wondered.

'Well this has been fun.' She drained her beer and stood up.

'Ain't it just.' Americans weren't supposed to do irony. She left the rest of the beer, and the candle. He sat up a good while longer, smoking.

For a fun weekend trip, try the riverboats on the Mississippi. Or the shops in St. Cloud are really neat. She still hadn't bought a map, had no idea how close she was to either of these places. Mrs Kieser's handwriting was tidy and rounded. Mr Kieser wrote, in block capitals, terser missives. *Turn Faucet off hard. It drips.* That night she could hear it dripping, padded downstairs in her slippers and dressing gown and tried to shut it off. It dripped on. She put a sponge under the tap and went back up to bed.

On the Sunday she worked through her notes, on the porch. There was no movement from the house next door, no sound. When the phone rang it startled her. She wasn't sure if she should answer it or not. Nobody had her number here. In the end she picked it up, cautiously.

'Kieser household.'

'Oh hi, honey, how are you doing?'

'Er, this is not Mrs Kieser. The Kiesers are in England.'

'I know that, honey, it's me. Marge, Mrs Kieser. I just thought I'd call, see how you were doing. Don't worry, it's not your bill. Fred bought one of those call card things.'

'Oh. I'm fine. The house is fine.'

'We just love your darling little house. Don't we, Fred?'

'Oh. Good. And I like yours.'

'Very good. That's great. Well, we just called to check everything was OK. Fred says – what did you say, Fred?'

Fred rumbled in the background. Mrs Kieser murmured back, muffling the phone so Lucy couldn't make out any of the words.

'Fred was wondering do you have a drier?'

'Oh. No.' Lucy thought about the way her underwear stiffened on racks hung over the radiator. Her cups drying upside down beside the sink. 'There's a clothes line, in the garden.'

'We know, it's just darling. But it's a little damp just now.' Lucy wanted to apologise abjectly to the Kiesers for everything. The weather. Her lack of appliances. The pinched narrowness of English life. Instead she gave directions to the laundrette. Mrs Kieser thanked her profusely. The laundrette would be neat. She closed the connection between them with an efficient click, leaving Lucy to the hum of the wires that separated them.

Lucy said down the phone to the dial tone, 'I worry about your neighbour's kid.' Perhaps she should leave them a note.

Lucy sat in the library and read the long-dead letters of the long-dead poet whose archive had been bought by the University. She tried to ring the colleague's friend but his voicemail informed her that he was out of the office until September. The poet wrote about love and courage and cheated on his wife. He idealised the children he'd abandoned. That morning she had got as far as picking up a phone book, but she didn't know what to look up. At home it would be the social services, child protection. Here, she didn't know the names. And besides the kid was clean, healthy, well fed. Lucy tried hard not to notice if he was being left alone or not. He ran around the yard on sturdy legs and sang. In heaven there is no beer.

Lucy shook the words out of her head and concentrated on the letters she had requested from the archives. One, the crucial one, was missing. It was listed in the request form but when she asked, the librarian made a show of consulting Lucy's brandished printout and shook her head.

'That one's in conservation. It won't be out until the conservator comes back, in the fall.'

'But I'll be gone by then. I just want to make a quick transcript. Please.' In Lucy's mind the letter became the key to her whole research. The missing piece. The librarian smiled the pleased smile of an official who knows she is right.

'We take conservation very seriously here. I couldn't interfere with the conservator's decision.'

Lucy had become accustomed to the can-do helpfulness of the Midwest service culture. She had grown used to having her gas pumped and her groceries bagged. For waitresses and car park attendants and shop girls, nothing had been too much trouble. So now, faced with intransigence, she backed down. The librarian tapped one more time with her long lacquered nail on the printout.

'Not till the fall.' She smiled her painted smile. Her teased hair did not move a millimetre. Only her eyes shifted slightly under Lucy's gaze, sliding sideways and down at the printout. Lucy requested another letter, an inferior letter. She lacked the courage to challenge another's brazen confidence. She retreated to her seat in defeat.

Lucy went around the house closing up the windows against the coming storm. The prairie flowers had been flattened against the wind as she drove up the highway. The radio talked about tornadoes in the St. Cloud area. She wondered about those neat shops, and how close they really were. Mr Kieser had tackled the note about tornadoes. *In the event of a Tornado open the Windows. Go into the Basement.* Her knowledge of tornadoes began and ended with *The Wizard of Oz.* Maybe she should be opening the windows, not shutting them. The radio rattled off place names but they meant nothing to her. Thunder was growling somewhere. She opened the door carefully when she heard the bell, fighting it against the wind. It was the neighbour.

'Is it a tornado?'

He laughed. 'Nah, that's a ways up north, up St. Cloud way. But listen, I got to go somewhere. And Tyler gets frightened with the thunder.'

'He can come here.'

'Oh no, he's in bed already. All I need is someone to sit in the house, be with him in case he wakes. I'll be back real soon.'

She could hardly refuse. At least he was getting someone to babysit for him this time. She picked up a book, the poet's book.

'Appreciate it.'

She nodded. He roared off in his junky brown car. She looked in on Tyler who slept, eyelashes dark against his cheek.

When the rain came down it came in sheets, roaring off the porch roof. She wasn't dressed for the cool air the storm washed down, but she sat on the porch anyway, lit the citronella candle, and watched the shadows dance against the walls. Her book sat on her lap and gathered insects. They crawled across the poet's words. Courage. Love. With a sudden impulse she slammed it shut and killed them all, smearing them against the pages.

Lucy had grown used to the way cars crept around the suburban streets. The sudden screeching halt of the long low car in front of the house startled her. She stood up to confront the angry blonde who clacked up the path in the rain.

'Who are you?'

'Who are you?'

'I've come for the kid.'

'Tyler?'

'He got any more kids in there?'

'He's asleep.'

'I've come to take him.'

Lucy sighed. 'I don't know who you are. Mr . . .' she realised she didn't know the neighbour's name. Didn't even know if he was Tyler's father. 'He didn't say anything about someone coming to pick him up.'

The rain had turned the blonde's hair into rat-tails. 'I'm his mother.' She climbed uninvited up on to the porch. 'I've come to take him home.'

Despite the rain dripping on to her shoulders she had the varnished confidence of the librarian. Lucy looked around her. Hadn't this been what she had wanted? But there was something in the clicking impatience of this woman's fingernails against the handrail that disturbed her. Lucy had been sitting at her desk in the library that very morning, laboriously copying in pencil the ramblings of the poet when a single sheet was slapped down beside her. She had recognised the footsteps, the defiant heels of the librarian, in a place where all the scholars crept in rubber soles. She picked up the sheet. Her missing letter. Turned her head to see if there was some explanation, some apology forthcoming. Saw only a self-righteous retreating back.

Lucy found her courage. 'I'm sorry, but I can't let just anyone march in here and take Tyler. I don't know you from Adam.'

'Who's Adam? And who the hell are you?' The blonde flung open the front door. 'Tyler!'

'He's sleeping.' But Tyler came slowly down the stairs, a step at a time, clutching a rag of blanket.

'Mommy?' He stood at the bottom and didn't approach either woman. After that one word he was silent, watchful, grave. The blonde didn't approach him either, simply looked to Lucy in triumph. Lucy remembered his heart-turning smile. She folded her arms.

'He's not going anywhere until' – she wished she knew his name – 'he comes home. He left me looking after Tyler and that's what I'm going to do.'

Lucy, the blonde and Tyler sat, in silence, on the porch. Tyler slept, one thumb in his mouth, on Lucy's lap, the lap he had chosen. Lucy turned the pages of her book and pretended to read. The blonde, tense as a strung wire, watched the street. Suddenly she stood up, flounced down the path towards her car.

'I'll be back.'

'Try in daylight next time.'

When the neighbour returned Lucy said nothing to him about it. She handed him the warm curled weight of Tyler, the rag of blanket. He smoothed Tyler's hair, and hefted his weight to one side, pushing open the door with his hip. From one hand a six-pack dangled. Lucy took back her citronella candle and returned to the calm blank luxury of the Kiesers' life.

*   *   *

A few days later, her research done, Lucy got up at that early hour inhabited only by insomniacs and fugitives and international travellers. For the last time she stepped into the Kiesers' car and pulled out of the drive, past the shut-up quiet of the sleeping houses. At the airport she parked in the long-stay car park, put the parking ticket in an envelope on the notice board, and posted the spare keys to the address that had been hers for a month. She would have passed the Keisers somewhere over Canada, but too far away to wave.

Back in London the next-door cat greeted her with an ankle-twisting display of welcome, implausibly claiming not to have been fed for a month. Lucy lifted the kettle and heard the familiar susurration of limescale around the element. She let the cat settle on her knee as she sat down, her hands cradling her first cup of tea, and gazed out at the shine of rain-damped leaves. The cat's weight, transmitted through kneading paws, seemed suddenly insubstantial. She found herself singing as she waited for the tea and the cat to warm her bones. A slow song, psalm-like, in a minor key. Embellished with whistled variations. In heaven there is no beer.

LYNNE TRUSS

Good Dog

THE EXPERIMENT of the dog took place in the early 1950s, when my family – consisting of Mum, Dad and Helen – was in its new and rudimentary phase, all black and white and Box Brownie, and still charmed by the postwar novelty of domestic possibilities. I wish I had known them then, this optimistic nuclear group in their new council house with a calipered sapling outside. This was their time of milk and honey, you see. Material for Mother to make little school frocks for Helen; carpets, electric light, internal lavatory; a horse-drawn cart delivering coal; endless new jobs available for Dad, for when he got fed up and walked out. When Mum collected Helen at a quarter past three from the new redbrick infants' school, they would often come home to find Dad full-length on the sofa (a sofa!) with the dog on his lap, asleep. Dad was still feeling his way into life after the army. In the civilian world, you could try things out, couldn't you? However big a mistake you made, it wouldn't kill anybody.

By the time I came along, the dog had gone, and had left no trace. In fact, when Helen first told me about the dog, I assumed she had invented it for her own self-aggrandizement, as was often the case with my big, big sister. Contrary to all the evidence, Helen believed she was a misplaced member of the royal line who would one day lie down in her

Clarks sandals on a pile of mattresses in Bentalls Department Store, sense the presence of a tin of peas beneath, and be revealed. Cleverly, she made me believe this too – although I have to say my parents never fell for it. So it was only natural that while she awaited the inevitable Slumberland Test, she filled the time just practising being superior to the rest of us, and in subtle but persuasive ways blaming me for the collapse of the house's fortunes.

'We had a beautiful pedigree greyhound before you were born,' she told me one day when I had been doltishly admiring the sleek rump of a chestnut boxer called Lady. I remember I didn't believe her. A greyhound? Ours was so obviously a dogless home. My mother couldn't stand dogs – on the beach at Ramsgate she would throw away rock buns that had been within five feet of a dog's livid, drooling open mouth, and if a dog approached her, she would let out a fearful whimpering, as if about to die. 'Are you sure?' I pressed Helen. 'Of course. Her kennel name was Nanette of the Knights Templar, but we couldn't call her that in public, for fear of people stealing her. So we called her just Nana.' 'What was she like?' I'd ask. But I knew the answer. She was a fine, exquisite, noble dog. Boxers called Lady might be good enough for me, with my childish low taste, but if a dog was to be Helen's, especially if it wasn't real, it had no choice but to be the last of the Romanovs.

But Helen wasn't making up Nana. True, there was no trace of her – no old collar hanging poignantly from a nail in the meter cupboard; no sense in our little dark hall of a long-ago echoing woof. But there were two pieces of photographic evidence I found in the shoebox in the utility sideboard, confirming Nana as a fact. In one picture my younger slimmer father, in baggy civilian turn-ups and with virile rolled-up sleeves, crouched in long grass on a sunny day, smiling, fag in mouth, and hugged the slender dog around its neck. In another, an uncertain group of permanent-waved Bethnal Green aunts in unflattering spectacles and print frocks stood outside our house front, its lawn still a dirt patch, its bricks bright and dark. Dad and Helen crouched in the foreground with the dog. You could see Helen's knickers. She looked incredibly happy.

One of my mum's favourite expressions was 'What you don't have, you don't miss.' Forty years later, I write it down and realize for the first time it is in all likelihood the stupidest saying in the world. But it seemed to make sense when I was small, in the early 1960s when we no longer had a dog and my parents had come to welcome every setback as a convenient excuse not to try anything again. For example, we tried beetroot once and it stained a tablecloth. We made a costly excursion to the South Kensington museums and failed to find them. 'Well, she's the expert!' Dad exploded, meaning me. On the way to Littlehampton I was sick on the coach. We went out to lunch with an uncle and I got stuck in the lavatory. On each occasion, it was the same. 'Well, we're not doing that again,' my mother said.

But somehow, the beetroot and the museums did not loom as large for me in their absence as the dog. My favourite handkerchiefs had dogs on; I chose as my best friend the girl whose dog was Lady; I saved my pocket money for a novelty alsatian nodding-dog – even though we didn't have a car. And for a form of family recreation so weird and reprehensible that I now thank God no social workers made speculative visits in those days, I would beg my sister Helen to pat me on the head, hard, while I knelt on all fours on the nylon rug in front of the fire and made doggy panting noises with my tongue out. When Tolstoy wrote the famous line about unhappy families all being unhappy in their own peculiar ways, was he, I wonder, picturing a scene like this? Helen, baffled but gladly obedient to my wishes, saying 'Good dog' and bashing me square on the head; me saying nothing but 'Harder!'?

I suppose I felt the home needed a dog again. After all, how had we lost Nana? Was it my fault? It was unlikely that the Knights Templar had spotted her one day in the bed department of Bentalls Department Store patting a tin of peas about and with a flash of crusading sword reclaimed her. I saw Nana as perhaps simply too well-bred to live long in the tawdry modern world I represented: so, in the elegant pose of a medieval wounded hart, Nana ascended – to chase forever the mechanical rabbit at the celestial dogtrack in the sky. The idea that she was a bad dog, a nervy dog, a woofy physical stupid dog who caused arguments, and had therefore been given away within three months of her acquisition, was a possibility beyond my apprehension. To me, a dog meant a family had love in it. Which was why, I suppose, during the summer holidays when I was nine, I overstepped the mark with both Lady and the Babcocks.

The Babcocks were my friend Christine's family. They lived on the same street, in an end-house like ours but with all the rooms the wrong way round. I spent so much time in their mirror-image house that sometimes, at home, I would walk into a wall where I thought a door ought to be. But the Babcocks were not our mirror image: they were, I see it now, like us before I was born. Christine's parents were young and dynamic. They grew vegetables and tolerated other people's children. It was at their house that I had beetroot and heard about museums. I shelled peas and played badminton. Christine's pretty mum worked at a garage; meanwhile her dad showed me how to let myself in to their house – a key on a string inside the letter-box.

Personally I liked standing on their shiny oxblood doorstep, ringing their chiming doorbell in ingenious ways, though I now suspect that this uncalled-for ding-dong virtuosity was the very reason I was told to use the key.

So the act was not premeditated. Coming in from the garden, I had been worried to find Dad on the old sofa in the usual between-jobs position, and instinct told me not to stick around. Stable employment was one of those things that certainly did seem to be missed by our family, even though we'd never had it. So I went to see Christine, pulled the key through the letter-box, opened the door, and found myself alone in their house. I knew at once the family was out, from the frightening stillness in the hall. It was a warm day and all the windows were closed. I stood and waited, while my ears sang. I knew I should let myself out, immediately; go to the swings; go to the library. But I didn't have my loan cards or my Milly Molly Mandys, and couldn't go home to get them. Through the living-room door I spotted Christine's modern ranch-style doll's house, with its bright plastic paradise flower garden, abandoned in beguiling disarray on a chair. And in the corner of the room, on a very hairy blanket, exuding deeply doggy smells, was Lady.

I had never touched Lady, I ought to explain. I was, in fact, terrified of her. Though I always struggled to control my shameful reflexes in front of the Babcocks, real dogs in real proximity generally caused me to make the same cowering movements and point-of-death whimpering noises as my mother. The Babcocks rough-housed with Lady; threw sticks for her; swam with her in lakes; told her she was beautiful and that they loved her. Now, as Lady watched me in the quiet house, panting, from her oddly soiled blanket, I felt acutely that I wanted to be a Babcock. I yearned to have Lady love me, too. So, 'Hello Lady,' I whispered bravely. 'Lady!' Her ears pricked but she didn't move. Lady's chocolate-brown eyes rolled in her sweetly ugly furrowed face; she snuffled and lolled her flat wet tongue over her sharp yellow teeth.

Helen and I stopped doing the 'Good dog' routine after that. Considering the risk of brain damage I had been running, this was undoubtedly a positive development. In any case – as had now been explained to me a number of times – even a 'good dog' will turn on you when she's a bitch on heat cornered by a stranger on her own territory. Lady did not savage me when I thumped her on the head and said 'Good dog'; I moved too quickly. But having been provoked, she leapt and snapped, which was enough for me. I sat in the Babcocks' kitchen wailing with shame; wailing with obscure but profound self-pity; wailing because Lady didn't love me, that I wasn't Helen, a misplaced royal, and couldn't remember Nanette of the Knights Templar, or the time when Dad had hugged her in the sun. When the Babcocks came home and found me exhausted and hiccupping in their kitchen, they could not piece together what had happened, but knew they didn't like it and that they didn't want me in their house again.

So that was it with dogs, for me. There wouldn't be a next time. I put my dog hankies in a drawer and gave the nodding-dog to a Canadian girl at school as a surprise going-home present – which must have been quite a big surprise, actually, as she wasn't going home. Helen was nice about it all. She could afford to be. She was a tall girl in the sixth form by now, and somehow certain to come into her true inheritance pretty soon. She told me that once, before I was born, Nana snapped at Dad, the way Lady snapped at me. 'Poor Nana,' I gasped. I knew what it felt like to be a bad dog, a very bad dog. My heart ached for Nana's disgrace. 'No, the thing was,' said Helen, 'he was different in those days. Everything was different then. He forgave her because he loved her!' And then she cried because the story was so beautiful.

Obviously there were lessons to be learned from the whole Lady experience. Mainly the lessons pointed in an inevitable direction: I wouldn't be trying that again. I remember Mum asked if I'd like to go to the Horse of the Year Show but I looked up from my Enid Blyton *Rub-a-Dub Mystery*, calculated my chances of ruining it – being sick, getting stuck in the lavs, being flatly unable to direct everybody to Earls Court – and said no thanks. And I could see I'd said the right thing: Mum seemed relieved. Meanwhile those kindly Babcocks, quickly relenting after their initial shock, urged me to come out on picnics with Lady and make friends, but I said it didn't matter. I wasn't a dog lover any more. I loved Nana, but secretly. Nanette of the Knights Templar. In my mind she was a good dog, a very good dog; a very, very, very good dog.

And one day towards the end of the summer, we went swimming together at the baths – Mum, Helen and I – and we had quite a nice time, indicating that we might even attempt the experiment again. True, we might leave it until next year, but it was a definite possibility. But when we all got veruccas, I was honestly as relieved as everyone that the swimming had been the usual self-eliminating disaster. One more experiment crossed off for ever. One more thing that, not having, you didn't have to miss.

ANNIE KIRBY

The Wing

NINA HÄGERSTRAND dreamt that something black fell over the school.

'Like a big, black wing,' she says, wiping a smear of pistachio ice-cream from her chin.

Nina and Callie, shiny in their patent leather shoes and the red coats made with fabric salvaged from *A Midsummer Night's Dream*, are sitting in the ice-cream half of Joe and Gianni's ice-cream-parlour-cum-barber-shop scooping up Gianni's special Pistachio and Turkish Delight with fan-shaped wafers. The sunlight filtering in through the arched windows is fan-shaped, too, dancing around the edges of Callie's pageboy bob. Their red coats are nearly matching, except Elsa Hägerstrand added scalloped flaps to the pockets and I used the white mother-of-pearl buttons from my wedding suit.

'Don't be silly, Nina,' I say. 'Eat your ice-cream. Quick, before it melts.'

'My throat's ever so much better,' says Callie, the corners of her grin twitching over alternate scoops of pink and green. 'I think I'll be able to go to Show and Tell.'

There's a smudge of black dust on Callie's brow and I wipe it away with my thumb. When Callie was Mustardseed and Nina was Titania they'd had wings made out of coathangers and pantyhose.

* * *

The Mazzini brothers came to Battstown in spring, when the tulip trees were in bloom. Joe was the older, quieter brother, in charge of the barber-shop side of Mazzini's. He had broad shoulders, a straight nose and a single, audacious streak of white hair like a badger. I liked his slow smile and large hands, hands that looked too big to cut hair. Best of all, he wasn't a miner.

Getting Joe was easy. I took him a canary, in a little gilt cage with a swing and a mirror.

'You have to have a canary,' I told him, as he brushed hair away from Nils Pedersen's collar. 'It's practically the law in Fallam County.'

It was nearly the truth. It had started as a joke, one that Grandpa Tyler used to tell sitting in his porch on Grant Street, something to do with canaries and miners. Now everybody had one and Bob Jacobsen who ran the pet store had bought a Chevy Nova convertible with powerglide transmission.

'I shall call her Lena,' said Joe, coaxing the bird out of its cage to perch on his finger.

'It might be a boy,' I said. 'It's hard to tell.'

George Johnson jangled into the store for his two o'clock appointment and Joe wrapped his hand around the canary to stop her flying away.

'I can feel her little heart beating,' he said.

'Did you bring a canary for me, Lena?' Gianni was leaning hip first against the sliding partition door that separated the barber-shop from the ice-cream parlour, an abstract pattern of blackberry stains on his apron.

Joe blew, ever so gently, on the canary's chest, ruffling her feathers.

'Little Lena will sing for us both,' he said.

Not long after that, I stopped being Lena Roberts, miner's daughter, and became Lena Mazzini, barber's wife.

Joe is shaving carefully around the edges of Gil Gilbert's sideburns and Gianni is washing glasses for the knickerbocker glories, hurling friendly abuse at his brother across the open partition, the way he always does. I'm jittery, my fingers trembling as I trim Martha Patterson's bangs to just above her eyebrows. I wonder how Gianni can be so calm.

'It's longer on the left, Lena,' says Martha. 'What's the matter with you today?'

We feel it before we hear it. It shudders up through the linoleum, through the soles of my impractically strappy sandals, into my ankles and knees. My scissors bounce off the metal arm of Martha's chair with a dull clink. Then comes the noise, an endless, pulsating rumble that makes my temples throb. Gianni drops the glass he is drying and I see it shatter and spray out across the partition divide. See it, but don't hear it, because nobody can hear anything any more.

There is a moment of total, utter silence. I press on my ears, to see if they are bleeding. Joe is motionless, the razorblade still between his fingers. A line of blood is blossoming along Gil's cheek, curling pink through the shaving foam.

I run out into the street. At first, I think there's been an explosion at the mine, the light is so bright. But it isn't an explosion. The reason there is so much light is because the mountain that usually casts a shadow across Battstown is gone. I stand there stupidly, not able to comprehend what I'm seeing. The top of the mountain isn't the only thing that's gone. A river of black dust and sludge has flowed over the school.

*   *   *

Gianni was in charge of ice-cream. He was the reckless brother, the artistic one. He had wanted to be a sculptor, or a poet, or a dancer but Joe had persuaded him there was big money in frozen confections. So Gianni directed his creative talents into ice-cream and became a master. Amaretti coffee, chocolate hazelnut, chilli pepper, vanilla almond, raspberry swirl. Gianni's cactus fruit sorbet raised eyebrows from Fallam County to East Liverpool.

It was hard to believe they were brothers. Where Joe was leisurely, measured, meticulous, Gianni was fizzing with energy, quick to laugh, short-tempered. He let his hair grow wild and curly in a town where anything longer than a number one meant you were a queerboy. All the girls in Battstown wanted him anyway, but he didn't want any of them. Or, rather, he wanted them all, but only temporarily.

In the mornings, I washed and cut ladies' hair, mixed tinting lotion and swept up hair and coal dust. In the afternoons, I served ice-cream in glass dishes and wiped coal dust off the countertop. In the evenings, I bleached and starched white towels and tablecloths. My hands grew cracked with bleach and perm lotion. Coal dust burrowed into the fissures, tattooing my knuckles and the soft skin between my thumb and forefinger with root-like patterns of delicate blue lines.

'My sweet, little Lena,' said Joe, stroking his fingers through my bob. 'Perhaps we should curl your hair, to encourage more custom.' He blew into my scalp, his breath hot, but he couldn't blow the dust away.

'Don't,' I said, twisting my head out of his grip. 'I have to see to Callie. Can't you hear her crying?'

It isn't a real mountain, the one that's fallen on the school. It's a coal waste tip, a black mountain formed out of things that were supposed to stay hidden underground. It's been here for so long we all think of it as a real mountain. Now there's just blue sky, beautiful blue sky.

Nearer to the school the newly released sunlight is shot through with miniature whirlwinds of black dust. It gets into my eyes and throat as I run and I'm already coughing when I fall down into it, screaming Callie's name. Gianni grabs my arm, closes his fingers tight around it.

'Go and ring the bell, Lena. We need to get the miners out of the pit.'

But someone has beaten me to it and the bell starts to ring anyway.

'I need help, Lena.'

Gianni was sitting on the countertop, five glass dishes of ice-cream in a neat line. He kicked his heels against the formica.

'If it's help with ice-cream you want, ask Callie.'

'Callie's palate is not, how shall I put it, refined enough. She will adore them all and make herself unwell.'

'Ask one of your girlfriends, then. I'm sick of ice-cream.' I smoothed the final linen tablecloth over the last table, ready for the next day's trade.

'I'm asking you. Come here.'

I relented, reached out for a spoon. He brushed my hand away.

'Close your eyes please, Lena. This is to be a blind taste test.'

Gianni folded a freshly starched napkin across my eyes and tied it behind my head, his fingers moving through my hair. He pushed a spoonful of ice-cream into my mouth. The coldness leached into my teeth and temples.

'Macadamia nut and white chocolate.'

'Very good,' said Gianni, 'but what do you think?'

'Too sweet.'

'Take a sip of water. What about this one?'

'Peanut butter and banana. Not sweet enough.' The bright whiteness of the blindfold, the cold metal spoon, eating ice-cream standing up, it was all thrilling somehow. Reckless. I could hear Joe's slow steps in the apartment upstairs. 'Cinnamon, apple and walnut. The one you made last month was creamier.'

Gianni dabbed ice-cream from my lip. 'I forgive you, Lena.'

'Forgive me for what?'

He reached around the back of my head and unknotted the blindfold.

'For not bringing me a canary.'

They bring the eighth graders out first. They were playing baseball in the yard but didn't have time to run. Gianni joins one of the digging teams, rivulets of coal dust and sweat running down his white tee-shirt. He is still wearing his apron and now coal dust mingles with the chocolate sauce stains. I haven't seen Joe, not since I ran outside leaving him standing with the razorblade in his hands. Watching the rescue operation is like watching a movie with the sound turned down. It's chaos, hundreds of people digging, crying, searching, listening. Yet everything is so quiet.

There's a muted cheer when they find the first ones, until we realize they are all dead. I watch in numb silence as the miners carry the bodies out one by one. I'm certain Callie's still alive, trapped in an air bubble, crouched beneath her desk. I hope Nina is with her.

I see Gianni carrying a body, a child. He doesn't look at me.

* * *

32

It went on for months, a year perhaps, the seduction by ice-cream. In the end, it was I who broke the stalemate. *Happy Days* was on upstairs and I could hear Joe and Callie's laughter wafting through the thin ceiling.

'I love Joe,' I said, spooning marshmallow and vanilla semifreddo into Gianni's mouth.

He swallowed. 'I know. So do I. Try this one.'

'No.'

His smile dipped a little. 'No?'

'I've had enough ice-cream.'

He folded his arms and looked at me. Kept looking at me.

I kissed him. I leant across the table and kissed my husband's brother on the lips. It was a chaste kiss by most standards, but I parted my mouth at the end and tasted marshmallow and tobacco on his tongue.

We did it right there, to a gale of canned laughter from the TV upstairs, the pristine, white tablecloth crackling underneath me, my stilettos denting the leatherette stool.

Later, when I was lying next to Joe, I tried to listen through the wall and hear the sound of Gianni's breathing. Joe moaned and turned over in his sleep, his white streak of hair luminous in the glow from the streetlamps.

They lay the bodies out in the chapel. We push the pews to the edges to make space. One of my sandals is broken but I don't remember how it happened. I limp up and down the neat rows of bodies, searching for Callie. The bodies are black with dust. They line them up a grade at a time, more or less in height order, so it's like looking at Russian dolls. I want to scream, but there is no sound in me.

I go back up Main Street, thinking they will probably be bringing Nina and Callie out soon, sole survivors, Callie clutching the rag doll she made herself and took to school for Show and Tell.

It's the most beautiful day of the year so far. Sun and breeze lick through my hair and the branches of the tulip trees are crowded with greenish-yellow flowers. Gianni is sitting on the sidewalk, his face swirled with dust and sweat.

'We missed our bus,' he says. 'It left . . .' he wipes dust off his watch with his apron, 'fifteen minutes ago.'

His body starts to shake, as if he's either laughing or crying, but I can't tell which.

'Stop it,' I say. 'Just stop.'

'We shall go to Venice,' said Gianni, rubbing his thumb around the lace edging of my garter belt. 'Or Rome, or Milan. To England, if you like.'

'Callie would like to see the Leaning Tower of Pisa,' I said, 'and perhaps Trafalgar Square.'

I shivered, partly from the cool breeze that rippled through the cemetery, mostly from Gianni's hand on the silky inside of my thigh. I liked the burning sensation of it there, branding our intimacy into my skin.

Later, when I was pressing towels and tablecloths and dreaming of piazzas, frescos and gothic cathedrals, Joe twisted a strand of my hair between his thumb and finger.

'You've styled it differently,' he said. 'I like it.'

I held my breath, the place on my thigh Gianni had touched still flaming.

'Don't forget Jodie Anderson is coming in for her tint tomorrow.' Joe kissed me on the neck, blinked, turned away.

I look for Joe in the barber-shop, as if he might still be standing there with the bloodied razor in his hands. I need to change my broken sandal but I can't face opening the packed suitcases hidden under the bed upstairs. I left the address labels on the cases blank because, after Boisville, we didn't know where we were going. The bus tickets were for yesterday but I made Gianni change them so Callie wouldn't miss Show and Tell.

I find Joe in the chapel. Mothers are running up and down the rows of bodies, searching for their children. There are bodies of adults, too, teachers and people who'd been in the wrong place at the wrong time. Gil Gilbert is counting bodies, *thirty-five, thirty-six, thirty-seven* and tallying them off in a grid in his notebook. Even with the grid, Gil keeps losing count and having to start again from the beginning.

Joe has folded his large frame into the ground and is kneeling beside the body of a child, a boy. I don't understand what he's doing, not at first. He's cleaning the boy's face with a wet handkerchief. When Joe has finished he combs the child's hair with his best salon quality comb. Joe takes his time, carefully smoothing out all the tangles, his thick fingers moving gracefully through the dead boy's hair. Enough black dust comes out so that I can see he'd been blond. It's Peter Hallstrom, and underneath the coal dust his face is blue.

'Lena.'

It takes me a moment to grasp that Joe is talking to me.

'I need more water. And towels, bring me some towels.'

I want to laugh then, out loud like a lunatic, because what Joe just said makes it sound as if he is about to deliver a baby.

'I can't find Callie,' I whisper.

'No,' he says, gently, keeping his eyes on Peter's face. 'They haven't brought her out yet.'

Upstairs in the apartment I grab tablecloths by mistake.

Out of the bedroom window I can see the cemetery where Gianni and I made love, glimmering as the streetlamps stammer on. There won't be enough room, I think, for all the bodies.

Lena, our fifth or sixth canary, is in her cage, twittering to her reflection. I close the curtains and she hops up on her swing to sleep. It's a game Callie loves to play, closing the curtains against the sunlight in the middle of the day and sending Lena the canary to bed. In the ice-cream parlour, somebody, Joe I suppose, has switched off the freezers and Gianni's creations are melting in colorful puddles across the floor.

On my way back to the chapel I see Tabitha Simpson wandering across Main Street in her pajamas and my stomach rolls. She's in Callie and Nina's grade.

'Tabitha,' I shout, 'Tabitha, did you go to school today?' but she totters right past me in a daze. I snatch at her arm, nearly dropping the bundle of tablecloths.

Tabitha starts crying, but she can't speak. She's caught the laryngitis that kept Callie off school last week. Tabitha's momma Claire runs out of her house and gathers Tabitha up. Claire Simpson keeps her eyes down, can't look me in the face. She must know she'll have no friends left in this town, just like poor Tabitha.

Joe and I wash the faces of dead children. We know them all, through haircuts and ice-cream. We wash faces and comb hair all night until they bring Callie out. Gianni carries her into the chapel, kisses her forehead and lays her down next to Nina. He touches Joe's shoulder, but Joe doesn't look at him. Joe washes Callie's face with a clean tablecloth he's saved just for her and I comb her hair, part her bangs the way she likes them. If her face wasn't so blue she would look like she was asleep, dreaming.

'You should have taken her,' Joe says, softly. 'You should have taken her yesterday like you planned.'

He starts to unpick Nina's pigtails, so he can comb the dust out of her hair.

Gianni is waiting outside, leaning against a tulip tree. He puts his hand around my wrist, the way I like it.

'There's nothing here for you any more, Lena.'

I want to tell him he's wrong, that everything is here now, but I'm too empty for words. I unwrap his fingers, prizing them away from my arm. The bright disc of his cigarette dims as the sun rises and floods into the space left by the fallen mountain.

It takes me by surprise, the sun coming up. It doesn't seem right.

→ Joe knew they were going to leave

→ Icebems
→ form + structure
  ↳ analepsis (flashback)
  ↳ present

CARYS DAVIES

Hwang

FOR THE past three-quarters of an hour, I have been sitting here in the coffee shop of the Barnes & Noble bookstore on Diversey Avenue with Ellen, as I do every Tuesday morning between ten forty-five and eleven thirty. Inevitably, we have been talking about Hwang.

I first met Hwang on a Monday afternoon five years ago, the spring Peter and I arrived here from Cleveland. He was living then, as he does now, with his old mother and his beautiful daughter in a tiny apartment on the corner of Diversey and Clark, a short distance from our house.

He is a small, lean man of indeterminate age. He could be forty, he could be sixty, I don't know. Every day he is dressed the same: the same pair of black felt carpet slippers, the same loose wool trousers suspended from a crumbling leather belt, the same threadbare khaki shirt with short limp sleeves and one breast pocket. He never smiles. His fingers are scaly and curled like a cockerel's toes, he has the quick, searching neck of a lizard, the watchful face of a cruel emperor, a ruthless bandit; the face of a person you might go to for the execution of some stealthy but vicious crime.

Hwang is my dry cleaner – mine and Ellen's – and I have been going to him now for the best part of five years, usually twice a week. Once on a Monday afternoon to drop off Peter's shirts, once on a Friday morning to collect them.

Other items – Peter's suits and ties, my blouses, dresses and skirts – I usually take in with the shirts unless there's some emergency on another day, something that's been forgotten or that needs doing in a hurry. In which case I make a special trip in the middle of the week, maybe two. Mostly, I would say, I am at Hwang's at least three times a week.

A few people in the neighborhood prefer not to use him. They think he is scary and rude, which is true. He is probably the most frightening and offensive person I have ever met.

Generally you go in, your arms laden with the week's cleaning, and stand there for a full two minutes while he ignores you, face wearing its permanent mask of furious scorn, carrying on as if you weren't there, shuffling back and forth in his tattered carpet slippers, sorting piles of laundry on the counter, throwing shirts into the giant wheeled hamper behind, dry cleaning items into a mountain on the floor; other items needing repair he hurls in the direction of his ancient mother, who sits in the corner, dressed entirely in gray, crouched over a dressmaker's sewing machine and an enormous rack of at least a hundred spools of different colored thread.

When he is ready, you are allowed to put your dirty laundry on the counter. His system is no different from any other dry cleaner in the neighborhood, no different from any other dry cleaner anywhere, really: one ticket for you, a copy for him to keep with your laundry to identify it when it is ready to collect. Hwang's tickets are pink and he keeps a pad of them on the counter, next to a dish of wrapped boiled sweets which I think he puts there for the children – though, as Ellen says, show me the child that would dare reach up under Hwang's assassin's glare and take one! When he has checked your things into the appropriate piles, he fills out your pink tickets (separate ones for laundry and dry cleaning) in his jagged scrawl, tears each one from the pad with a sharp, brutal twist of his bony wrist, and thrusts them in your face. In my case he usually barks *Flyday* at this point.

When I return on Fridays for Peter's shirts, or in the middle of the week for any other oddments that are ready, I hand Hwang my pink ticket, or tickets if I have more than one, and he shuffles off into the back, muttering and truculent, under the racks and racks of cellophane-wrapped garments, each one labelled with one of his duplicate tickets. When he has located your things, he brings them to you without a smile, and impales your old ticket on the sharp spike he keeps next to the bowl of boiled sweets. I have often pictured him, as he does this, in the stony yard of some village, wringing the necks on a row of shabby chickens, though I have come to realize I might be wrong about that.

The worst thing about Hwang – much worse than the not-smiling and the grumpy shuffling about in the felt slippers – the thing that most appalls people, the thing that frightens some of them away completely, is what happens if you lose the pink ticket he has given you.

'No Ticky,' he says then with vicious finality and something like triumph. 'No Shirty.' Clamps his little mouth shut, folds his ropy arms across his limp khaki shirt, and glares at you. A proud, challenging, disdainful glare it is impossible to ignore.

It has happened to me before now, and it has happened to Ellen. In fact when it happened to Ellen, a couple of years back, Hwang practically reduced her to tears. He stood there repeating that hideous rhyming couplet of his while she balanced her purse on her knee and hunted through it for her ticket, which wasn't there. When she begged him to try and find her things without the help of a numbered ticket Hwang just stabbed the air with his cockerel's claw, indicating the row upon row of garments hanging from the ceiling awaiting collection, as if inviting Ellen to dream up a more impossible task. Eventually, that time, he did give way, puffing and sighing and making a huge fuss of rustling all the clothes in their cellophane covers as he looked through.

These days, he is less obliging. He has become much worse about this business of the tickets.

What brings people back to Hwang in spite of his rudeness, is that he is cheap – at 99 cents a shirt he is cheaper than anyone else in the neighborhood – and his work is excellent. Also his old mother, sitting wordlessly all day in her little corner, carries out repairs and alterations of the highest quality; invisible mends like healed skin.

And then there is Moon.

Hwang's beautiful daughter.

It is worth going to Hwang's just to gaze for a few minutes at Moon. She is now, I would say, about sixteen years old. She has a broad, exquisite face, hair the color of a raven's wing, cut to her chin. I've said to Ellen many times that if Peter and I were ever to change places, if I were to go downtown every morning and spend the day behind his gleaming desk at First Boston and he were to collect his shirts from Hwang's on a Friday afternoon when Moon was in there doing her school-work, he would never come home again.

Moon wears the navy and forest green uniform of one of the private Catholic schools in the city: pleated plaid skirt, green wool blazer, white blouse with a piped Peter Pan collar which always looks as if it has been starched and pressed that very morning by Hwang himself.

There are a handful of such schools in the city, where the discipline is strict, the education narrow but reliable, where uniforms are worn and the fees are relatively modest. Still, you can see what a struggle it is for Hwang. How he glares at that laundry hamper with its 99-cent shirts inside. Hwang looks as though he will die in his slippers paying those fees so that Moon won't have to run the shop after he's gone.

We have been talking about Hwang and Moon, this morning, Ellen and I.

We have both noticed them lately, arguing in the shop. Moon looking sullen and rebellious and not sitting down at the table in the corner next to her grandmother where she is supposed to do her homework. Hwang pointing a curled finger at her books and making himself look even uglier than usual with all this shouting at Moon. Looking as if he is telling his daughter that he hasn't crammed his soul into his threadbare khaki shirt, his crumbling leather belt, so that she can grow up to become a dry cleaner. One terrible scene I witnessed ended with Hwang throwing the bowl of boiled sweets up into the air, along with a whole pile of pink tickets snatched up off the spike on the counter. The sweets bounced across the floor and out across the sidewalk into the gutter, the tickets floated about in the steamy shop like butterflies and even the old woman looked up for a moment from her work in the corner to see what was going on. Then Moon ran off in tears through the curtain in the back, up into the tiny apartment above.

Ellen and I discuss Hwang's ambitions for his daughter, and end up agreeing that with her grave, exquisite face, her raven-wing hair, she looks so much like a fairy-tale princess that ambition and hard work may not matter for her, because *someone* is surely bound to come along one day, and whisk her away from the chemical smells and the drone of her grandmother's sewing machine and the damp kiss and sigh of her father's steam press.

Ellen is my friend.

She has been my friend ever since the day Peter and I arrived here five years ago, ever since the spring afternoon she came across the street from her house to ours, bearing a tray of iced tea and three white saucers of Pepperidge Farm cheddar cheese Goldfish, one saucer for each of us. She has lived all her life in the neighborhood, grew up here and lived here with her husband Norm until he died of cancer nine years ago. The day after we moved in, she came back over and took my arm and walked me around our little area here, where I have come to feel so much at home: the small but adequate A&P the two good hairdressers; our dentist, Dr. Sandusky. The Barnes & Noble bookstore with its coffee shop, where I have coffee with Ellen every Tuesday morning, where I am having coffee with her at this very moment. The Ann Sather café where Peter and I go for a pancake breakfast on Saturdays. There is the Swedish butcher; a chiropodist; a medium-sized Walgreen's; four small but thriving theaters the three of us attend whenever there is something showing which appeals. The hospital and medical centre are only four blocks from our house. There is Hwang too of course, less than three minutes' walk away, and the branch library where I attend a book group every third Wednesday in the month and Ellen comes across to cook Peter his supper and keep him company.

Peter has promised me we will never have to move again; we've moved so much over the years with First Boston, and I have found that as I've grown older, settling into a new place is something I do increasingly badly. I did it worse in Cleveland than in Atlanta, worse in Atlanta than in Philadelphia and everywhere worse since the children left.

It has been different here. I have found I have everything I want; all my needs seem to be looked after in this half square mile with all its now-familiar places. I have Peter, and I have Ellen, and I have always felt that there is nothing else in this place I could possibly ask for.

Much of my conversation with Ellen revolves, inevitably, around the neighborhood. Speculation about whether the new extension to the Ann Sather café will be ready by the end of the summer. How much longer it takes to find what you want in the A&P since they changed everything around. I tell Ellen which book has been chosen for the next meeting of my Wednesday library group and from time to time I try to persuade her to come along with me, at which she laughs and throws up her hands so her silver bangles slip and clatter along her arms, and says, 'What! And have Peter starve?'

We wonder about the funny smell from the roadworks at the intersection of Clark and Lincoln where they have dug up part of the sidewalk in front of the dental surgery, about how the new young man with the red hair at the Swedish butcher's might have lost his thumb; and at some point on these Tuesday mornings, sooner or later, we end up talking about Hwang or his old mother or Moon.

The other week I said to Ellen that Hwang reminded me, with his baggy wool pants and his ruthless lack of mercy, of a ninja. A ninja about to pounce.

Ellen hooted at this, threw up her hands. Her silver bangles clanked. 'A *ninja*! Hardly, Sal! Ninjas are *Japanese*. You can't think Hwang is *Japanese*!'

Ellen was almost choking with laughter, fanning her hand in front of her mouth so her bangles started clanking again.

'*Korean*. He's from *Korea*. All the dry cleaners here are Korean now.'

She said that when her mother was a girl here they were all Jewish owned; now it's the Koreans; one day, she said, it will be another lot.

Ellen was a schoolteacher once and very occasionally she can still sound a little like one; she can sound ever so slightly lecturing.

'No,' she repeated, still chuckling, '*not* Japanese.'

I shrugged. 'I know that, Ellen.'

For a moment we were silent, Ellen took a bite out of whatever kind of cookie she was having that day, a sip of coffee.

'He still makes me think of a ninja,' I said.

In fact, I had always thought Hwang was from China. Or rather, I'd never really thought much about exactly where he was from. I'd wondered why he is the way he is, so bitter and angry and haughty. I'd wondered if there was a Mrs Hwang, if perhaps she had been too frightened to come here with him and start a new life in America, if she might still be over there somewhere, if Hwang was still trying to send for her. I'd wondered, also, if he had perhaps once occupied some position of rank, if that accounted for his brutal disdain, his bullying rudeness, the impression he gives of so much swallowed pride. Of bitterness, maybe, at the way life has betrayed him, or been so hard.

Perhaps his difficulties with Moon are getting him down.

I don't know.

What is certain is that over the years that I've known him he has grown angrier, more frightening, meaner to his ticketless patrons. Where once he would eventually shuffle off, with a lot of bad-tempered mumbling, to search through all the hanging clothes for the items in question, these days he will not budge. He just stands there behind the counter, shaking his head and looking mean; obdurate as a stone.

I have always liked Barnes & Noble for coffee. The green paint and brown wood are soothing, the plush carpet is soft underfoot, there is an atmosphere of quiet repose, and the cakes are good. Today I am having a tall latte and a slice of cherry crumb cake, Ellen a lemon cookie and a decaff espresso.

She is wearing a fawn linen pantsuit and a cream cotton blouse cut square across her collarbones. A print scarf around her throat – she doesn't like her throat, she says no one our age should go out with her throat uncovered. She looks well-groomed, rested, at peace. She looks exactly like herself.

It is six days since I came back from the library and found one of Ellen's silver bangles in our bed and I can think of no sensible way to proceed. I am frightened of speaking, of saying a single word, either to Ellen, or to Peter. I'm certain that if I put anything of what I feel into words, I will poison the air we breathe and none of us will ever recover. I have become increasingly certain over the past week that the best thing to do is to say nothing, to let things run their course. To stay quiet until whatever is going on has come to a close; to hope for some kind of invisible mend.

When we are almost ready to leave, Ellen says she won't be a second, she just needs to go to the bathroom. I watch her get up, thread her way between the little round tables. At the first bookcase she turns back, points back at her chair, mouths, Watch my purse a second?

Ellen's Cole Haan purse, boxy and black with two tall handles, is sitting upright on her chair. The shiny leather is cool to the touch. The zipper makes almost no sound. There is very little inside. House-keys. A hairbrush. Chase Manhattan checkbook in a navy blue plastic case, a single lipstick, her maroon wallet. I fan my thumb across the checkbook stubs looking for I don't know what. The lipstick is nearly finished, its scent powdery and delicious, the scent of Ellen herself. In her wallet she has forty-five dollars and some loose change. A receipt from the One-Hour Photo on Clark Avenue, a pink drycleaning ticket.

There is one last mouthful of cherry crumb cake left on my plate. I pick it up with my fingertips, put it in my mouth. Then I eat the dry-cleaning ticket.

It is, I know, a small, stupid thing to do.

I know also that I might just as well have crushed it in my palm and dropped it into the metallic swing bin over by the cakes, or just slipped it into my jacket pocket – it's very unlikely Ellen would ever have found it in either place. But sitting here now, thinking of Ellen's silver bangle, the shock of it against my foot, eating the ticket seems the only available thing to do. It is almost impossible to chew, it skates between my upper and lower teeth like the squeaky scraps of articulating paper Dr. Sandusky has me bite on when he's checking a crown or a new filling. In the end I munch it into a ball and with one painful swallow it's gone and all that's left in my mouth is the sharp, inky taste of Hwang's bitter scrawl. A picture in my mind of Ellen, rooting hopelessly through her purse. Hwang behind the counter, arms folded. His pugnacious fury, his proud, frigid grandeur. Fixing her with his ninja's glare.

TARA GOULD

The Turnover Bridge

UNDER THE old turnover bridge Caspar Bliss holds up his top in a roll above his nipples to let the sun warm his bare stomach. He runs his palm over the flesh to get a sense of living. He is a lean man, the muscle is like tyre underneath the skin.

He watches as the sandy hairs spring out from under his fingers, looks at the water half in light and half in shadow, then shuts his eyes.

Two boys are fishing from the canal further along. Uneasily they watch the tall man exposing his tummy. He is half in shadow and half in light, under the bridge, cut through diagonally. He has a very straight back and his bottom sticks out like a child's. One of the boys whispers 'Paedo!' to the other, and they look at the man and then back at the tiny ripples that constantly reproduce around the green and blue feather float. The nylon line pierces the patina like a needle.

Caspar, eyes squeezed tight shut, is unable to stop thinking of his date last night. How she'd flung her head back and laughed when he told her his name. She had a lot of fillings, one or two brown teeth, but he still fancied her. She got him to buy her drinks all evening. He accompanied her home on the bus. At the end of the journey she'd said of course it had nothing to do with his name, he just wasn't her type, she was looking for someone more . . . *dynamic*.

Caspar lets his top fall, takes out a pen and a note pad from his back pocket, and writes on the paper.

There were six years of pain at school after his mother changed his name, and all because of the Christmas play. It was the first year he had secured a part. He had played one of the Magi. *Enjoy the show*, the Head had said to the huge audience. He had tried to fill himself with presence, like his mother had taught him, he could hear people laughing but his mother told him his performance was *luminescent*. He tears the page out loudly and looks around him. Two boys further down the canal turn quickly away. He pushes the folded page into a crack in one of the old red bricks, then he walks towards them.

'What time's your dad coming?' one of the boys says loudly as the man approaches.

'Any minute now,' the other replies.

Last night, he'd wanted to tell her that it *was* because of the name, really. Even a police uniform had not given him the natural air of authority he had always craved. The sort of authority that Richard and Graham had had over him when they made him get down on all fours and lick the soles of their feet.

He stands behind the boys, mousy-haired, one darker and straighter than the other; they are unyielding.

'Morning,' he says.

'. . . Morning,' the boys say *sotto voce*, still staring at the tiny ineffectual ripples that emerge and withdraw around the float.

'I used to come fishing here as a boy too, nice spot really. . . . Caught anything?'

'Not yet,' say the boys, unable to ignore an adult.

Silence, and the sudden sound of a bird alerting in the tree behind.

'I know you think I'm a perv, but I'm not, okay. I'm a policeman. My job is to catch pervs, not be one,' he says and he takes his proof from the pocket of the jacket he is carrying, and holds it out to the side for them to see. The wavy-haired boy nudges the straight-haired boy. They indulge the stranger, *Constable C. Bliss. Bedfordshire Constabulary*. The photograph shows a man with blue, almond-shaped eyes and an uncertain grin.

'So, you can relax.'

The boys laugh nervously and twist round to look up at him, their young clear eyes twinkling and squinting against the sunlight. 'Oh, no, no, we didn't, we didn't think that,' they are saying with unbroken voices, words overlapping.

Caspar smiles down at them, the smile of someone who knows, but who forgives. But the smile lacks warmth. It is a strange and tight smile, he feels it. He watches the boys rotate politely back to face the water, which is turning brown as the sun slides behind a cloud.

'I don't know how fish could survive in here any more, with all the shit they dump,' Caspar says. He notices the semi-opaque plastic container full of maggots nestled in the grass next to the straight-haired one. The lid is on, but he can just make out the writhing mass within.

'My brother told me they put the fish in,' the straight-haired boy says, more relaxed now. 'This is his gear. I've never done fishing before. It's our first time. He's been going on about it for years. We thought we'd give it a go, but I don't see what all the fuss is about. It's quite boring.'

'You need to go with someone who knows what they're doing. How long you been here?' Caspar asks.

The wavy-haired boy looks at his watch, '"bout three hours, since six.'

'You've got worms *and* a float?' Caspar asks, looking at the green and blue fly stirring gently on the water as the straight-haired boy shifts his position.

'Couldn't get the maggot on,' he says, 'did my head in.'

They watch an approaching narrowboat. *The Benevolence* is written in black and white on the side. A large man in a white shirt and orange shorts steers. Three generations of women, all with differing tones of bleached hair, an inch-wide black line at the roots, sit drinking coffee and smoking cigarettes. The water licks the olive velvet of the mossy concrete canal sides, and the blue and red boat slowly motors past.

'That's one of the Wyvern Shipping Company's narrow-boats,' Caspar says to the boys suddenly, in a voice a bit too forced. 'They've got three. They hire them out now, for day breaks and holidays but they used to carry coal along the Grand Union all the way from the Coventry coalfields to London. Timber as well.'

The boys follow the narrowboat out of sight, until the engine can no longer be heard. A slight breeze pushes at their faces, parts their fringes and rustles the leaves in the tree behind. Then, for an instant, the wind falls flat and settles inert on the ground, and there is total stillness.

The wavy-haired boy picks some grass and sprinkles it on the water. But it does not drift, it gradually makes its way back to the concrete side directly in front of where the boy sits.

'We came on a field trip down here with my school last summer and did all that. The way of life of the boat people, the industrial revolution and stuff,' the wavy-haired boy says. 'All I remember is that that bridge is a turnover bridge,' and he gestures to the bridge Caspar had been standing under.

'Can you remember why?' Caspar asks like a teacher.

'No!' the boy deflects.

'Something to do with the horse crossing over,' the straight-haired boy answers nonchalantly after a pause.

'That's right. It allowed the towing horse to cross the canal without the towline getting caught up in the bridge. *Smooth* curves.'

'Why did the towpath have to cross sides?' asks the straight-haired boy. Caspar pauses, 'I don't know . . . something to do with ownership . . . I don't know . . . ownership of land . . . possibly . . . or the lay of the land, steepness of the bank. . . .' He stops abruptly and crouches behind the boys.

'I used to come down here all the time when I was a kid, used to watch the water, sometimes the sun setting in the water, when I was upset. Watch the water, it's calming . . . I used to walk along by the river as well, through the Ouzel meadows that run between. It's got quite overgrown over there now, since they decided it was a bloody nature reserve or a place of ecological significance or whatever it's supposed to be. Some places you can't even see the water, they've let it all go wild, chaotic. What's the point?' Caspar says but the boys do not respond because he seems unnecessarily upset. The wavy-haired boy gets a whiff of his breath, he shuffles forward.

Caspar watches himself stand awkwardly and take a step back and then suddenly the wavy-haired boy is tugging on the rod.

'Reel it in, reel it in!' the other boy shouts, and the line is wound in. A fish the size of a medium carrot swings back and forth in the air. The flecked skin seeming to roll in the sunlight, oily but clean. They pull it to them, bringing in also the damp, irony smell of the canal. The straight-haired boy takes the hook out tentatively, his chin jutting forward and his tongue out. He gently lays the slapping body on the grass.

'It's a perch,' Caspar says.

But the boys do not respond. They look at the fish for a while, curling and twitching, and when its movement lessens the straight-haired boy picks it up and throws it back in, as if it were a skimming stone.

Caspar watches two writhing maggots in the grass beside them, ridiculously bright like wedding dress silk in the sunlight.

'Goodbye then,' he says, raising his hand.

'Bye,' the boys reply. They watch him as soon as he turns his back and paces away, back into the shadow under the bridge.

The boys begin to pack away their things. When they look again the man has gone. Another narrowboat comes past. It is blue and purple and there are boxes with pansies on the roof, a pink bike and an old pushchair. Inside there is a woman with dark red hair hanging down her back, jigging a crying naked baby. There is a ginger cat trying to paw something out from the pile of logs at the front of the boat. The boys stand and watch.

'Cats normally hate water,' the wavy-haired boy says.

'Perhaps it was born on the boat,' the straight-haired boy replies to comfort himself. They pick up their backpacks and swing them on to their backs, deftly sliding arms through straps.

At the top of the Turnover Bridge, the boys pause to bend their stomachs over the warm brick wall and look down to where they sat. The grass is crushed and, just before the canal curves away out of sight, a coot unknowingly leaves a gathered line behind it and disappears into the reeds and overhanging bushes on the far side. The wavy-haired boy crosses the road and peers over the other side of the bridge. A white van comes, slows down, then beeps. The boys wave it over, there's nothing coming the other way, and it drives between them.

'There's that weird policeman,' the wavy-haired boy says and the other crosses the bridge and looks to where his friend is pointing. A yellow shirt and blond head bob up and down through the meadow.

'Do you think he really is a policeman?' says the wavy-haired boy.

'He had that card.'

'He could have nicked it off of someone.'

They watch as the bobbing head gets smaller and darker.

'Come on!' says the straight-haired boy and they run down the left side of the bridge, jump over the stile that enters the meadow and hurry along the thin path through the long fluttering grasses where flying insects softly rise and move on.

Caspar arrives at the river and ties his jacket around his middle. He crosses the six rough planks bridging the water at a narrow point over vines and weeds. They are not completely secure, they move as he steps over them. On the other side of the river he walks between ancient pollards, lime-green with foliage. He gazes up to the highest branches of a black poplar. He sits, resting his spine against the bumpy tree. He can see the river, there are two dragonflies bouncing over it, back and forth in a loop, making high arcs at either end. He shuts his eyes, listens: birds, buzzing that comes and goes, a breeze through the leaves above. But really, there is only the sound of the water. A deep, low hush.

The boys reach the planks.

'He's over there, look!' the wavy-haired boy says, pointing.

They look at the profile of the man, straight-backed against the tall, thin tree. The sun hits him through a gap in the branches and his hair looks golden white. They cross the planks and walk slowly along the river bank, stopping behind the nearest tree when the man opens his eyes and scans around. The wavy-haired boy starts to giggle.

'Shush!' the straight-haired boy says, 'he'll hear us.'

The man takes off his socks and shoes, rolls up his trouser legs and begins vigorously rubbing his calf muscles.

'What's he doing?' the wavy-haired boy whispers.

'How should I know . . . being a weirdo prob'bly.'

The man stands up and stretches his back against the tree, then walks away.

'He's forgotten his stuff,' the wavy-haired boy says.

'Perhaps he's going for a paddle?'

Caspar watches the river moving slowly past, the green and blue dragonflies. He sits at the water's edge and removes his trousers and his yellow shirt. He folds them and lays them neatly beside him. He watches the skin on his arm as the goose pimples grow like tiny pink horns.

The boys move closer and crouch behind a tree.

'What's he doing now?' says the wavy-haired boy, alarmed.

'How should I know?'

They watch as the man stands up and begins to remove his underpants. They are beginning to giggle uncontrollably as his white bottom is revealed.

'Shit, he's getting his whole kit off. Look how much his bum sticks out!' the straight-haired boy whispers through suppressed laughter.

'Do you think he can see us? Oh no, I think he's gonna flash.'

The man stretches his arms in the air and looks up to the sky. He then turns full circle twice and the boys see his ginger pubic hair and his light-brown penis. They hold their hands over their mouths to stop their laughter escaping.

'He's got fire wires!' says the straight-haired boy, and they shake, bent over double, hysterical.

Then the man slowly, carefully descends the bank, slipping clumsily on the muddy sides and letting out a terrifying groan as his body hits the cold water.

'He's only going for a swim . . . told you,' the straight-haired boy whispers.

They listen as the man splashes about, gasping and grunting, but they cannot see him. After some time all they hear is the sound of someone swimming up and down. Then, after some time again there is silence.

The silence continues. The boys listen, hearing only the scratching of birds and squirrels in the treetops above, the sun is warm on their faces. They wait, and the silence coming from the man continues. They wait.

'Let's go and see!' says the straight-haired boy.

'No!' says the wavy-haired boy, 'he might be waiting for us. He might ambush us.'

Minutes pass; still there is only the lurch of the breeze and the thick, whispered roar of the river.

'He's drowned,' says the straight-haired boy, and they look at one another, scared and solemn-eyed.

'Don't be silly,' says the wavy-haired boy, 'he's a policeman.'

Slowly, quietly the boys approach.

The man's torso floats face down.

His long legs disappear underneath, and into the dense brown of the water below. His back protrudes like a turtle shell, the muscles lumpy. The back of his head is covered in a green mesh of plants like a hair net. He is still. He is being shifted slightly, dreadfully, by the gentle undertow, towards the opposite bank.

'I told you!' says the straight-haired boy in a high voice, 'I told you he'd drowned!'

They stare, eyes wide, alert.

'No, he's not. He's just floating.' But the man is not moving.

'What shall we do?' asks the wavy-haired boy.

'Call an ambulance,' says the straight-haired boy and the wavy-haired boy takes his mobile phone from the side pocket of the rucksack and dials. They wait while seconds pass slowly and the man bobs, face down.

'I hope they get here soon.'

'We have to get him out!' says the straight-haired boy suddenly, 'or he'll die.'

The boys look at the weeds, the brown water, and at the quiet, big, horrible body.

'What if he's already dead?'

'He can't be. It takes longer than that to die. Surely it takes more than that to die.' And in a moment the straight-haired boy has his shoes and socks and trousers off and is clambering and slipping down the bank.

'Come on! Come on! We can save him.'

Caspar is sitting on the edge of the Turnover Bridge with a fishing rod, perched, as if positioned by somebody else, legs permanently bent like a garden gnome. But the bridge is under water and the fish are swimming under the bridge and right in front of his face. He catches a fish, but it is as big as his head. He manages to get it into his mouth and he swallows it whole but his insides are aching. The fish moves down through and out of him. He is crying with the pain.

Then he catches another and it is smaller. He sucks it into his mouth even without his volition, and again it travels through him, hurting less this time. He catches another smaller fish and puts it in his mouth. This time it swims down of its own accord, through his intestines, gently caressing, and out through his anus, making it tickle. He feels deeply contented. He drops his fishing rod and lies down on the warm brick wall, legs still bent under him. He begins to fall soundly asleep. A sparkling blissful pulse beats ecstatically through him. It is meant to be the last thing he feels, a parting gift, he knows that.

The man is heavy but buoyant, and the boys steer him quite easily to the bank on the opposite side. It is less steep, and less muddy. The man feels cold like the water. They still have their tee-shirts on. The wavy-haired boy is shivering and pale.

'Over here, over here. To this bit,' says the straight-haired boy.

They reach the flattest bank. The straight-haired boy climbs out and sits on the side. When the man comes closer to the bank the boy bends and pushes his wrists and arms under the man's armpits, and his legs either side of his torso. He feels the man's armpit hairs on his forearms. The hair from his head is lightly stroking him as it floats in the water. He is trying so hard to ignore these things, things that would normally make him laugh, or cringe, or show off or complain. He feels for a moment that who he is is not who he often thinks he is, or who he wants people to think he is, and it strikes him as the most grown-up thing he has ever thought.

'I'll pull, you push . . . *When I say*.'

'Where from?'

'Grab him round the waist or something, and try to lift him up.'

'One – two – three – NOW!'

The straight-haired boy pulls and the wavy-haired boy lifts but the man is heavy. They manage to bring the man's dropped head out of the water and up the bank about ten inches until the man's face pushes into the muddy grass, his features squashed.

'Again. One two three NOW.'

The man goes up another five inches, but his bottom half is still in the water. They rest and pant. They know they are not strong enough to pull him out, but they cannot let him go, or he'll roll back in again.

'Is he dead?' asks the wavy-haired boy.

'I don't know, I've never seen someone dead before. I can't hear him breathing,' says the straight-haired boy and the wavy-haired boy begins to cry softly and the other boy just looks at him and for a long time it seems that this is all that happens. But then the straight-haired boy also begins to cry because they are stuck half in and half out of the river having to hold the stranger's heavy body which might be dead and he doesn't want this to be happening to him.

In the distance the siren sounds. The boys look at one another and wait in silence; a tear falls from the wavy-haired boy's chin into the river.

'He's a policeman,' the wavy-haired boy says when the ambulance people arrive in their lovely green suits and take over the job.

'He's called Constable Bliss,' says the straight-haired boy as the man and woman gently but confidently pull him from the water. The boys scramble up the bank and wipe their muddy hands on their wet clothes. The dead man's face is like white putty, different to the one they remember by the canal.

The ambulance man gives mouth to mouth, and in between the woman pumps his heart. Constable C. Bliss coughs and splutters and vomits water as the woman pushes his pale tummy. He opens his eyes for a brief moment and scans the four faces. Eyes full of blood around the irises of pale grey, life still continuing. No surprise in his expression. No gratitude. The lids slowly fall and his head lolls to one side.

The ambulance man and woman lift the man and place him on a stretcher. They carry him through the meadow to the road and the boys follow behind. No one speaks. At the ambulance they load the man carefully into the back. The doors are closed. The ambulance woman takes the names and addresses of the boys before they leave.

'Well done,' she says, 'he may want to thank you.'

When the ambulance has disappeared around the curve of the road the straight-haired boy looks at the wavy-haired boy.

'Do you think we saved his life?'

'I'm not sure, I think we did.'

They sit on the grass by the road and they allow what has

just happened to take its place inside them. The adrenalin rush is being replaced by a feeling of heavy tranquillity. *This is special, we are special*, the straight-haired boy has in his head but not in words.

'I wonder what was on that bit of paper that he put under the bridge?' the wavy-haired boy says but the other does not respond and again they are silent.

'Do you think he meant to do it?' the straight-haired boy asks after some time, and the other shrugs.

The boys walk slowly towards the bridge. They are in no hurry to get to it, but they know they have to. Somehow this is their day too. It always will be.

In the diagonal shade under the dripping arch they stand exactly where the man stood and they feel like thieves.

The piece of paper is quite clearly there, sticking out from a crack between old red bricks, dampened with a little moss. The straight-haired boy tugs at it and unfolds it slowly for them both to see. It takes a while to register; they read it over and again. It simply says (in small neat capitals at the bottom of the lined page torn from a notebook, a policeman's notebook?), *ENJOY THE SHOW*.

BRIDGET FRASER

Threads

ANEES PICKED her way through the wheat straw, gathering it into bundles as she went. Their winter fodder
stack was growing but not fast enough. Soon the rains
would come and any straw still lying in the paddy field
would be ruined.

In the next patch, Sita moved quietly back and forth,
threading cottons from five spindles back and forth along
her bamboo framework. Slipping the threads over a stick at
the end of a row, she unravelled more and retraced her
steps. Back and forth, back and forth, for as many daylight
hours as their other chores permitted, Anees and Sita
worked near each other in the fields, sometimes stopping
to chat or share a joke or a bit of remembered gossip. Or
just to rub their aching backs. For five years now, Anees and
Sita had worked together: out in the field, Sita threaded the
warps, back at her home, Anees would weave them on her
loom. They shared the small profits from selling the finished
lengths of red and white shameez in the market. Their
informal partnership was good and saved them both the
endless haggling with the wholesale buyers over how many
days it should take to weave a length of cloth, how many
rupees the market traders would pay, when would they pay.
This way, they produced the finished work, ready for sale,
no middle men, no one dictating terms.

Behind Sita, her black bristle pig snuffled along the line of quilts airing in the sun. It settled to scratch its rump against the charpoy where Sita's husband lay sleeping in the shade. He woke, yelled at it, grabbed a stone to chuck, shouting across to Sita to kill the pig or at least pen it up then fell back to his sleeping. Anees glanced across the road towards her own house. Where was Manu? Would he have remembered to cut the kohl rabi for market in the morning or would last night's rice beer still be clouding his dull brain? With a sigh, she bent her back again to gather more straw.

On the roadway above her field, a shiny jeep bounced along then stopped and reversed. Doors slammed and Anees looked up to watch two people, not Indian, and their guide scramble down the dusty bank and on to the path leading to Sita's field. Shading her eyes, she watched as, with hand movements and much laughter, they tried to understand what Sita was doing.

'Come on, honey, come and stand with me and this nice lady, let's have a photo done,' a woman with large blonde hair called to her husband. Sita was enveloped into their circle and the guide took the required photo. By now, Anees, always glad of a diversion, had wandered across her field towards them. She took in their good clothes, the like of which were never found in the stalls or markets here, their clean, white trainers, their flashy shoulder bags. Wealth gleamed from them; they were as blinding as freshly gilded statues. Anees adjusted the sari across her shoulder and smoothed her skirt piece, conscious of her dirt-filled nails but still curious to get close and observe these rare visitors. The woman flashed large teeth at her in a smile of welcome. Anees felt like a visitor in her own field.

'Gee,' said the woman, reaching forward to touch the

fabric of Anees's skirt piece, 'that can't be muga silk can it? Real muga? And she's wearing it out here? In a *field*?'

Hashim, their guide, quickly translated part of the question for Anees. Anees stood a little taller and responded to him in her local Assamese dialect.

'Yes, this is real muga . . . but it is old now, it has holes in it.' She hesitated. 'It was part of my mother-in-law's dowry. You know? When she married?'

'Isn't that just so romantic,' sighed the visitor when Hashim translated again. Anees, a little bemused by the reaction, smiled in agreement anyhow. Anxious now to keep the visitors' attention, she glanced at Hashim and added quickly, 'But it is not my best. I have others.' Sita, still holding her spindles of thread in her hand, looked at her friend but said nothing and went quietly back to her work.

'Come,' said Anees, tilting her chin a little higher, 'I invite them to my home. Show them my loom and my weaving.'

'Really?' The large teeth flashed when the invitation was translated, 'that would be so great. Come on guys.'

'Please,' said Anees, 'follow me.'

With an elegant turn of her hand, she signed them back towards the dusty path. The unlikely trio, two upstate New Yorkers and Hashim, set off behind Anees, across the paddy fields. They scrambled up the bank back on to the road and crossed to the village. The small house Anees shared with her husband, daughter and mother-in-law was near the edge of the settlement. As they approached she called out: 'Manu! Manu!' After a few minutes, her husband, wearing a torn vest and roughly tied dhoti, appeared from behind the grubby curtain which served as their door, scratching his scrawny neck and yawning. As he focussed on his wife and her illustrious visitors, his mouth fell open then he fled back behind the curtain. The next time he appeared he was wearing a striped shirt and trousers. He rushed to bring stools for the guests and seated them on the swept earth patch, their front porch.

'Bring tea,' he ordered Anees. 'You will take tea?' he enquired.

'Sure, that would be great but we've only come to see your wife's weaving. And you speak English!'

'Yes,' he boasted, 'I was very good student at school. Show them your loom,' he ordered.

Without a word, Anees settled herself on the bench. Her shuttle flew back and forth, weaving threads of white and red, creating the traditional patterns of the shameez which she had learnt at her mother's knee.

'And what is this she's making?' the man enquired politely. 'Not a sari, I guess?'

Anees stopped the rhythm of her work and went to reply but Manu burst in:

'No, not a sari! This a shameez. The men wear it. Around our necks, you know?'

'Oh, I get it. A scarf?'

'Maybe so. We call it the shameez.'

Anees resumed her work in silence.

Manu had sent their daughter to fetch water and set it to boil. He fussed around, directing her to bring a low table, set with a cloth before their guests. The small front porch was getting crowded. Anees spoke a few soft words to her daughter in their dialect and very soon she brought a brass tray set with brass goblets, polished, shining, filled with freshly brewed tea.

'Ah well,' murmured the blonde to her husband, 'when in Rome . . .'

'Or in Assam, even.'

With smiles and gestures of thanks, they set to drinking their tea.

By now, other villagers had gathered just outside the woven bamboo fence which marked the home of Anees and Manu. They observed the ceremonies solemnly, without a word. Even the children were silent, watching as the visitors sipped their tea and smiled at their audience. They finished their tea, admired Anees's weaving and prepared to leave. Amid the small ceremony of farewells, the tall American man slid a 100-rupee note into Manu's palm. 'For your kids,' he insisted, 'and a small thank you for inviting us into your lovely home.' Manu joined his hands together in thanks before tucking the 100-rupee note into the pocket of his shirt. Watching from her seat at the loom, Anees knew exactly where that money would go: straight down his throat as rice beer.

As Hashim shepherded his guests back towards the jeep, he waved back to Manu. The gods were with him today; already he was planning another 'unscheduled' visit and counting on the enhanced tip he could expect from his guests.

Two weeks later Anees was working in the fields when she heard the cheerful toot of a jeep's horn. She saw Hashim waving to her from the road. She crossed the field to greet him.

'Chai?' she enquired. Hashim nodded enthusiastically and introduced Anees to his new guests.

'Come,' he invited them, 'let me show you how the yarn for our traditional shameez is prepared. Then you will have the opportunity to see this village woman weaving at her loom. It is possible you will take tea in a traditional village house.'

His guests, four of them this time, murmured assent and followed him towards the patch where Sita was working.

'But I only have two cups for guests,' Anees wanted to

protest, 'my husband is sleeping and I have work to do. The monsoon will come soon and the field must be cleared . . .'

But there was no chance to say any of this. Instead, she scrambled up the bank and hurried to her house. By the time Hashim and his guests arrived from the fields, Anees had sent her daughter to borrow two more good cups – not brass, but not cracked either – from a neighbour, and fresh water was set to boil for tea. Somehow, all four guests squashed on to her front porch, weaving was demonstrated and tea was served. Again, neighbours gathered to watch the proceedings. Again, as the guests departed, rupees were pressed into Manu's palm. This time it was 200 rupees.

'Two hundred rupees!' he crowed later to his wife as she cooked their rice and dal over the open fire. 'Do you realise how many hours I work to earn two hundred rupees?'

'But it is my weaving they come to see,' she reminded him, quietly. 'My weaving and Sita's work, too.'

'Ah! But it is my conversation. That and opening my home to them. That is what they pay for.'

Anees said nothing more. It was no use arguing. He would only beat her or, worse, break their few sticks of furniture in his rage. The last time that had happened, it was three weeks before he had mended the smashed leg of their charpoy. In the meantime, it was she, not Manu, who had slept on the hard earth floor.

Visits by Hashim became quite regular; once, sometimes twice a week. Always the visitors offered rupees by way of thanks; always they handed the small, grimy notes to Manu, never to her.

'I shall be a rich man,' he laughed, 'small farmer, big fortune.'

Anees continued with her weaving. Week upon week, she completed one length of shameez which she or Sita would take to the market. And so, by selling the cabbages and rice, mangoes or papaya, Anees kept her family fed as village women had done for generations. Her small surplus earnings went to pay for her daughter's schooling. Any extra, and that was little enough, she tried to keep hidden from Manu.

Visits by Hashim and his guests became almost commonplace in the village. Interest began to wane. Fewer villagers came to stare at pale-faced visitors from unimagined places from beyond their village, beyond Kolkata even. The novelty had worn off and no direct benefit had come to them – other than the small pleasure of seeing Manu ever more drunk and falling into ditches. But, beneath the palm leaf roofs and behind the flimsy mud walls of other huts, jealousy was growing. The discreet passing of rupees had not escaped envious eyes; the boasts of Manu had not gone unheard in the fields and in the mango groves where they all worked hard to earn a meagre living. Sometimes now, as Anees was drawing water from the well, other women would tease her that, soon, she would not need water, she could buy rice beer to drink all day. Or, worse, they would cease their village chatter as she came near and watch, in silence, as she filled her water pots. These were her neighbours. Together, they had shared their harvests, good and bad, the ceremonies and rites of birth and death, whispered to each other about the trials of men and marriage, shaken their heads in unison about the otherness of men.

Friday was market day. The villagers would rise before first light to harvest cabbages, kohl rabi, mangoes – whatever was in season and might earn a few rupees. Chickens, squawking, were packed into bamboo baskets and carried, live, the four kilometres to town. Some would find a buyer, have their necks wrung there and then; others would return to scratch a few more days of life. Wrapping their shawls about them, the villagers would set off in the chill dawn. Dogs, barking round their feet, escorted them to the village edge, skittering around the procession of old carts and bicycles. Babies, strapped in sacks to their mothers' backs, grizzled and sucked on milk-sop rags. No one dreamed of fortunes; survival was the only aim.

And then, one Friday in early March, a new sound interrupted the low babble of early morning preparations. One by one, the villagers paused from their tasks and listened, eyes narrowing. Without doubt, it was the burr and splutter of an engine. Coming closer, coming to their village. Quite soon, they saw a yellow and black auto-rickshaw hesitate at the palm trees then turn off along the track into the village. It bounced through the potholes, stirring up clouds of red dust. The dust and the rickshaw came to a halt outside Manu's hut. It pooped its horn. Twice. Manu appeared from behind the hut, struggling with a box of cabbages, two sacks of rice and one chicken in a bamboo cage. These he loaded into the rickshaw before shouting back to Anees. She refused to show herself so, with a shrug, he pushed past the few neighbours who had gathered to investigate the rickshaw and clambered in. The small crowd watched in silence as he set off, some children ran alongside to the edge of the village. One old woman spat with force into the dust.

Later that morning, Anees, her field chores finished, her pots cleaned, porch swept, sat working at her loom. The regular rise and fall of the frames, the rhythm of the shuttles beneath her fingers was not like work for her; it was a meditation. Many a woman's worries and tears were woven into a single length of cloth. She was so absorbed in her work that she did not, for a while, notice Sita standing just beyond the bamboo fence. When she did, she smiled in welcome, nodded to her to come in. Sita shook her head.

'I have come to say that I shall no longer thread your warps for you. We shall no longer work together.'

She turned and walked away, back towards her own hut before Anees could absorb the meaning of her words. For some moments, she sat staring at the space where Sita, her friend, her neighbour, her partner for five years or more, had stood. The space was empty but the words, 'I shall no longer thread your warps for you', still hung in the air like black crows.

A sentence of death would have been less painful. To be banished in this way, ostracised from the fellowship of her own community was unbearable. Slowly, she rose from her loom and went into the gloom of her hut. She lay down on the charpoy, staring at the palm leaf roof. The welling tears deepened into sobs of anguish making their mangy dog cower and howl beneath the loom while other women passed by on the other side of the track on their way to the well, keeping themselves away from her hut.

By evening, when Manu returned from market, flushed with pride from his ride in the rickshaw – to market and back again – but with no spare rupees to show for his day's work, Anees was cold with anger. No fire was lit, no water boiled for tea, no rice or dal simmered for his supper.

Manu paused outside the hut, trying to make sense of it all then shouted angrily for Anees. She failed to appear so he lurched inside, cursing as he stumbled against the loom, his brain and his eyes bleary with rice beer. Before he could draw breath to shout for her again, Anees attacked him.

'You fool,' she yelled, 'you stupid, stupid fool. I always knew I had married a stupid man. Only now do I see what a fool you are. I'd rather be dead than married to you. Get out! Out!' The sight of Manu before her, his mouth hanging open, enraged her further. She grabbed a cooking pan and ran at him. As he fled, she hit him on the back of the head. His yelps and her yelling had brought the neighbours creeping to witness the excitement. They were not disappointed. Oblivious of them all, Anees, wielding her pan, pursued her husband down the village path. No one offered him shelter or tried to stand in the way of Anees. Even after his hard day's drinking at the market, Manu could outrun his wife, hampered as she was by her sari. But still she pursued him, raging and shouting, cursing and abusing him. In her wake, small children and dogs joined in the chase. Villagers, the memory of Manu's rickshaw ride still fresh in their minds, watched and grinned wide grins, their betel-stained teeth lurid in the dusk of evening.

The next time Hashim called with guests, Manu was nowhere to be seen.

'He is tending the buffalo in the field,' Anees explained as she worked her loom for his guests before serving tea in her best brass cups. When they left, it was she who accepted their offerings of rupees, with grace and elegance and a folding of hands in *namaste*. The guests were enchanted. Hashim was puzzled but impressed by her presence. It was rare, unheard of even, for a village woman to take this role. Even so, his guests seemed more than happy. That could only be good news for him.

Waving farewell, Anees returned to her hut. She put one 50-rupee note into a tin hidden at the bottom of a bag of rice. The other she tucked into her sari to give to her friend, Sita, later, out in the field. Then she settled again at her loom where a fresh warp of red and white cottons was already threaded. More cloth to work before the daylight faded, new stories to weave into a new weft.

TREZZA AZZOPARDI

Remnants

HENRY HAD always had a thing about colour. His first ever memory, he told Moira, was of the paper sails his father hung above his cot.

If I shut my eyes I can still see them, he said, shutting his eyes as if that would prove it, Twirling in the breeze, Moi. There they go, now! Blue, and green, and red, and gold.

They'd just started courting. After hearing this description for the fourth time in as many dates, Moira felt the need to question his recall skills.

Wouldn't it have been yellow? she asked, What with the war on, I don't suppose there was much to be had in the way of gold.

Henry remained convinced of what he saw. Later in their relationship, aware of the fact that it wasn't really her role to disprove him, more confident, too, with the memory he had cultivated, Henry would describe these twirling sails as Azure, Moss, Scarlet, and Gold. Or, Cerulean, Sage, Ruby, and Gold. In the language of colour, he could accept no substitute for gold.

Thirty-seven years on, and when Moira heard him tell this tale, she no longer tried to correct him. But to the listener, she'd wink, or roll her eyes to the ceiling, and when Henry had finished describing his thing about colours, she'd add her own version of Henry's beginnings. The long one –

how on earth can a tiny baby remember such a fact? – would lead in to a discussion of what Henry could or couldn't remember as a fully grown man, including their anniversary, her birthday (never forgets our Catherine's though, does he?), when he last changed his socks, and who was the current prime minister. Or the short version – It would've been yellow, not gold, but Henry does like to emblazon.

If Henry had to describe what it was he did, he would say he accumulated bits of sunshine. He liked sparkle and texture, and kept, at the bottom of his garden, a shed full of items of bliss. There were nugget-sized flints from his lighters, their edges sharp and shiny like the teeth of some mythical creature; old brass fittings, door handles, knockers, and keys. He hid these joys from Moira. She believed that Henry had acquired a fixation for which they must find a cure. Her way of curing was brutal. The brass doorknobs, for example – which she insisted on changing for the new brushed aluminium that needed no polishing, and that to him looked dead on the door – she wanted to throw them in the bin. Henry rescued them, and lined them up, these dark, lustrous globes, in the far corner of the shed.

Henry worked in textiles, before the factory was rationalised and he was offered early retirement. He would have refused outright, but for the business with the curtains. It was such a little thing. The new fabric had been delivered a week before, and Henry watched as usual as the great curves of colour were wound off the rolls: row after row of lilac blooms on a soft blue background. It was his job to count the metres as they swooped past. Count the metres. He had never got used to it, and usually ended up guessing, estimating in feet and then doing a rough conversion on a torn envelope in the back office. He was more or less accurate. He was less and less accurate. The remnants stacked up in the dump bins like a gaudy reproach.

He thought the lilac offcut particularly pleasing. It would look marvellous in the bedroom. Moira could run the curtains up on her machine, and there might even be some left over for the window of his shed. He saw the remnant in the bin. He saw his hand as if it belonged to another man, reaching in, tucking the cardboard roll with the fabric on it under his arm, waving to Security as they arrived for their evening shift.

After they showed him the evidence on camera – no getting away from it, Henry, the camera never lies, the new under-manager said – Henry was offered retirement. He tried to refuse, but they made him sit down in the office and view the tapes. He saw a strange, grainy, too-fast image of a man, shot from high above so the sight of the fella made Henry run his hand across his head. He watched the man reaching in and walking away with a roll of red, a roll of green striped, a roll of lilac on blue. It was the same balding, stunted man each time, reaching in, over and again; a roll of red, a roll of green striped, a roll of lilac on blue. Except the tapes were in black and white. It was only Henry who saw the colours.

He missed his work days. Not just the sight of the fabric cascading like a ship's sail, but the delight in bringing a little something home. He loved to surprise Moira with his finds; it was better than giving her flowers. He brought her tiny swatches of Chinese silk; offcuts of carpet in emerald and tangerine; slivers of soft navy velvet which he wanted her to tie in her hair. Moira would raise an eyebrow, pointing to her salt and pepper perm, and the bit of fabric would go in the drawer with the rest.

All that was done with now, but the memory of the hues

and patterns sustained him. And at least part of that was with him still; there was colour in his days, even if Moira had turned out old and grey.

Moira feels choked. She drops the list from her hand and grips the back of the chair. How could she forget? She sits down, stands up again immediately. She can't remember now what it is that she's forgotten. She goes to the kitchen sink and leans against it, hoping it will come back. She takes a long tasteless drink, her head bent at an angle under the tap. She wanders through the house, two tiny beads of moisture clear upon her chin.

Henry was planning a new front room. It took careful consideration, hours of preparation which involved scrap-books and colour charts and swatches, and a tone-test area in the corner behind the television, where Henry tried out his colours in small squares: where Moira had to look at it whenever she watched *Emmerdale*. Moira called it his new fixation. Catherine said, with one eye on her mother,

Why not get the decorators in, Dad? You can get colour stylists now, even B&Q offer a service.

But it was his project; he'd seen the make-over shows, and no bloke in a frilly shirt, no girl in leather jodhpurs and her midriff showing was coming into his home to mock. They could keep their stripped bare this and their minimal that for people who knew no better.

Cumberland, Artex, Anaglypta. Henry sang a catalogue of trade names in his head as he strode towards the shop. Toile and flock, he added, jaunty with terminology. Henry wore his second-best jacket and the shirt Catherine bought him last Christmas. She would be coming for dinner to-night. He waved at Mrs Nix across the street, dropped in at the corner shop for some tobacco and a copy of the *Telegraph*. Happy Henry, in the sunlight.

The list says:

    Moira, please get –
    2 onions
    green pepper – or red if green not avail.
    celery (not from supermarket!)
    prawns (ditto)
    mush. 1/2 lb
    Do We Have Garlic??
    olives black AND green we have run out of both
    lemon (1)
    Back at 4
    H

Moira moves past the table with renewed purpose; she doesn't see the list. The draught from her body sends it drifting to the floor.

Cantor sensed Henry lurking at the door of the shop, and waited for the sound of the bell. Him again. He pulled open a ledger and studied it with feigned interest. From the edge of his vision, he watched as the old man ambled through the banks of patterned paper, occasionally reaching out with his fingers. Henry approached the far end of the counter and coughed.
    Just be a sec, sir.
    Cantor snapped the ledger shut and looked up with a flat smile. He drew on his shirt cuff with a pointed hand, knocking on the edge of the counter as if trying to remember something vital. Henry was looking up at the top shelf. A few wisps of stray hair rested on his collar.

Hello again, Mr Lasco. And what can we do for you today?

I'd like a look at that roll of blue, please. That one, no, no, that bright one there.

Henry directed him with a little nodding dance of the head. Cantor reached up, and a fantasy of striking the old man came from nowhere, sliding down off the shelf. He handed him the tube very carefully. Cantor knew that if he let him, Lasco would work his way along, colour by colour, until it was time for him to go home again. Henry clutched the bolt of paper.

It's nice heavy stuff, he said, weighing it with a frown. He saw it transfigured, an azure sea under the dado in the lounge. Cantor breathed in through his teeth. He put a hand on Henry's shoulder, retrieving the roll of paper from the other's palm.

If you'd like to look at our samples on the desk there, Mr Lasco? . . . or perhaps you'd care to pop in another day, when we're not so busy?

Henry looked around the empty shop. He turned back to face the young man. He would've liked to have told him how he remembered him in nappies, how he'd have a word with his father, how he needn't be so plain rude to a customer, but Cantor was smiling his dead smile. There was something in it that Henry feared. He moved to the door with a curt nod, feeling stupid, dry-mouthed.

He stood outside the shop. The sky looked too bright. The chime of the shop bell resounded in his ear. What would he do now, to pass the day?

It was the curtains she couldn't bear, especially in the mornings. The mess of carpets throughout – the green and yellow and orange that warred up the stairs beneath her feet – she could simply not look at, most of the time. She felt her way around the house like a blind woman, with her head high and a gaze fixed on nothing. But she couldn't escape the curtains. In the morning, the sun would splash the four walls lilac and purple, like a slow bruise breaking on the day. It was hard not to blame Henry for this. In her mind, the bedroom would be white. She had suggested it to Henry once, complaining of migraine from the colours, how it gave her a bad start.

White? he said, as if she had slapped him. White? as if she'd sworn. But he came home with a stack of colour cards to show her his white suggestions. Lime white, off-white, Hardwick white, old white, new white, wall white, stone white and bone white. Not one of them was white. Henry had done his best: only Henry could make a white not white.

Moira moves quickly now, no thoughts in her head, up the stairs, and along the landing to the bedroom. The curtains are still slightly drawn. She pulls swiftly at one corner, so fierce, her rage brings down the metal rail in a slice across her brow. Moira clutches the curtain to her eyes and presses on the pain. In the smell of tobacco and sleep, she finds stars. She wipes the fabric down her cheek, a sensation at once coarse and slippery. It doesn't absorb the blood.

After a while, she puts up a hand, and trails her fingers on the gash across her eye. It has an edge like cheese wire. When Moira finally raises her head, she sees light, flooding in, through clear glass.

Catherine, don't move! Stay where you are! Moira hears the panic in her voice and she feels it in her throat. She sees a small bare leg swinging from the tree.

Henry! she calls, as Catherine tumbles down. The child

appears to bounce into the earth. By the time Moira reaches her, she is tottering, laughing, slightly shocked.

I thought I told you to keep an eye on her!

No harm done, love, says Henry, bending down to rub the dirt from Catherine's knees. He takes out a clean handkerchief for the purpose, a show of solemnity which he knows his daughter will enjoy.

What on earth were you doing? Moira is glaring at Catherine.

I've got a present for Dad, says the child, holding up her bunched fist. Catherine opens her palm, and a yellow butterfly struggles into the air, bending on the breeze. They watch its path across the stubbled lawn.

Gold! says father and daughter together.

Moira stares through the window at the memory.

Henry turned off the road and cut through the archway down to the water. It was a fine, clean day. The riverside walk was sculpted in cream stone, the new black benches awash with drunks. Henry paused at the weir, where the rushing in his head could become a real sound. He spread his hands out on the iron rail. Catherine would come tonight. He clung to the image of her. He, too, always saw her as a child.

Here she is now in the garden, bent against the flat earth, her headband slipping back off her sleek brown hair. She is struggling to her feet, one hand cupped, the other bending towards her leg. He sees in her face that she's trying not to cry.

It feels to Henry just a moment's distance. He takes the handkerchief, bends towards her where her sock is grazed with grass stains and the imprint of elastic on her flesh is livid, and wants to kiss each tiny indentation on the skin.

Her small pink hand against the tan of his sends a lurch of grief through his chest. Catherine wouldn't cry, even with Moira standing at his back, daring her, almost wanting her to. She is her father's girl.

She would probably bring that stupid husband tonight. Henry put the thought away, cheered himself with the prospect of making his famous paella. They could open a bottle of wine. He saw the list of items in his head, and ticked off each one. He hoped Moira had managed to get everything this time. She was becoming forgetful. When he thought of her, the dryness in his mouth came back, spreading across the flat of his tongue. Who did she think she was, anyway, these days?

Moira stands in the stillness of the shed. She brushes a hand in front of her, imagining cobwebs. There aren't any, of course, all is clean and neat. Blinking in the darkness, her eyes scan the shelves in silent fury. She sees old fittings, jars of screws, numbered boxes, stacks of paper, coils of wire, a length of brown rope hanging from a beam. She sees nothing. It is very quiet. The shadows fall into her eyes, and Moira begins to think. She opens the lid of the toolbox, and draws out the claw hammer.

Reaching up with her free hand, Moira takes a jar of nails from the top shelf. It glides through her fingers, falls freely past her body and explodes on the stone floor. Her feet crunch against the shards of glass as she stretches up for another jar. She carries these items back into the house, the stream of crimson livid on her face.

The bent arm of the rail swings out proud from the window, the fabric hanging from it like a dying flag. Moira drags a chair across the carpet and climbs up to the square of light. She holds the hammer in her fist; she has two nails jammed between her lips. From here she can see the apple tree, just breaking into blossom, and a child's swing in the garden of number six. They never did build a swing for Catherine. He never did.

She doesn't hear Henry come into the house. He sees her first, a silhouette of bulk against the light. Her arm is raised, motionless. He's reminded of a statue of Saddam he saw in the *Telegraph* Travel section, a before and after piece. He almost laughs.

Moira is brimming with the memory of Catherine's youth, of her youth, and of white light. Her ears are filled with silence.

Henry makes a noise behind her, just a small puff of breath. But Moira knows this sound so well, has felt it strobing on her eye all day, beating a dark path through her veins. It has been travelling to this moment for years. He will cough, and then he will ask about food. He will not ask her how her day has been. He will question her about the freshness of the prawns, the provenance of the celery. Olives black AND green. Did you remember, Moi? Well, did you? – his particular finger of his particular right hand poking at the space in front of her. The rage is blinding. All is lurid colour, white noise, electricity.

She turns and strikes the shiny pond of Henry's head with the hammer, just once, just one good tap, and faces the window again. Her eyes search for the memory; it was so close just then. But it's gone now, it has run away like sand.

Henry falls gently on to the floor. He sees Moira's face, a harlequin of sticky brown and scarlet, the hem of her blue skirt, a spot of yellow sunshine on the carpet – no, not yellow, gold! – where his vision rests and stays. The rushing in his ear subsides.

Moira feels up to her cheek. Dried flakes of blood drift to

the floor. Her fingers are glittered with specks of red. She finds the two nails fixed in her mouth, amazed at how they got there. She has forgotten what it was she had meant to do, and glides down from the window, enjoying the whiteness of the light.

When Catherine arrives, it seems very important to tell her about the list. She shows her daughter all the things she has forgotten.

ROMI JONES

Eminem and the Virgin Mary

EARLY MORNING diesel trains wake you at dawn and remind you that you are living in an abandoned car. The inside of the red Ford Sierra is steamed up grey. You push open the car door and the shock of autumn makes you cough. Down by the railway track, you piss onto the weeds growing by the wire fence. Back in the passenger seat you light up the remaining inch of last night's spliff and plug in to the personal CD player they gave you for Christmas. The last present before they kicked you out.

The beat of the rap, the smell of the weed. Your head falls back on to the grey plastic of the car seat as Eminem takes over. *'Lose yourself in the music, the moment, the music, you own it . . .'* On the last drag of the spliff, the music stops. There is enough glow from the overhead lights on the railway bridge to find the Asda plastic bag on the driver's seat, search through papers and CDs to find the batteries that Benji gave you. When you put them in, there is still no rap. You feel a lump in your throat; you chuck everything on to the driver's seat and wait until it's time for the youth centre to open.

As soon as you walk inside, you know that Nicola is on duty because Madonna is blasting out of the stereo. You can smell toast and warm air and Nicola gives you a big smile. 'Hi Liam, marmite or jam?' She reminds you that she's coming with you to the meeting at Social Services at three o'clock. You empty the Asda bag onto the counter so you can try to fix the CD player. The bag smells of soap powder like the clean sheets at your grandmother's house.

Benji is going up the stairs and calls out 'All right Liam? Come round to my place later.' You watch him disappear into the interview room to see the counsellor. It must be Thursday because you can hear the market traders calling out in the town centre. You scratch the pimple on the back of your neck and feel the chain of the St. Christopher you have had since you were a baby. Maybe you should sell it but that might bring bad luck. When you check your pockets you find one pound and fifty-eight pence to last till social services sort out your income support.

At your feet, the local paper is on the floor; Nicola brings it in for the jobs page. You kick it out of the way because you're too dumb to read but you still spot the football score. Even your football team is losing.

You get comfortable on the brown corduroy sofa with your tea and toast, Nicola puts an Eminem CD on the stereo: '*Lose yourself in the music, the moment, the music, you own it . . .*' Mack comes in looking as if he has not seen hot water for a week. 'Eh Liam, what the fuck are you doing here?' 'Eating toast, Mack, just eating toast.' He says he is still waiting for the tenner you owe him and looks as if he will search your pockets himself before you can think of an answer. Nicola, five foot two and blonde, leaves the toaster and stands between you. Feet apart, arms hanging still by her side, she looks him straight in the eye. 'Mack, come back at one o'clock when it's quiet and I'll see you then.' Mack seems to consider punching Nicola in the face but instead he leans over till his nose is six inches away from her forehead and yells that he is pissed off with people fucking him about.

As soon as he's gone, you pick up your mug, still just warm, and spill your tea on your jeans. Nicola lights up a cigarette, leans against the kitchen counter and closes her eyes, inhaling long and deep. You ask if she wants a coffee. 'Liam if you are offering to make me coffee, that means you need a favour.' For a minute she reminds you of your mum; that same tone. As if she really wants to make everything alright for you even though you have probably got yourself into deep shit. You lean over the sink to fill the kettle.

'Thing is Nicola, my CD player is bust. I need a tenner to get a second hand one. I can't stand being in that car without any music.'

'Liam you've already had two lots of money from the emergency fund, a CD player is not an emergency.'

'It is for me.'

As the water tumbles into the kettle, you catch sight of the mirror above the sink. The black eyes and red face of the devil grin back. Last time this happened, you pulled up your hood, grabbed the coins from the petty cash tin and ran out the centre. You look again and he is still grinning; you drop the kettle, grab your bag and run into the street.

You can't stop running until you are down the back lane where the music shop is belting out Coldplay over the pigeons eating last night's chips on the pavement. Inside, you lean against the counter and ask TJ if he can fix your CD player. He picks up a screw-driver and removes the flat black plastic cover. 'Sorry Liam looks as if it's completely fucked.' He screws the back into place and passes it over the counter. You ask if he needs an assistant in the shop. He laughs and says he can hardly afford to pay himself, let alone employ staff. No customers; just you, the warmth of the shop and the rhythm of the music. You sit down on the wooden chair by the counter and close your eyes while the thrumming keyboard takes you some place above the roof-tops and below the clouds.

When you open your eyes, there are a couple of teenage girls in the shop, flicking through the racks of CDs. Both in school uniform, white shirts hanging out over their black trousers, ties loose around their collars. You search the lost continent of your childhood for the time when you got your first school uniform, remembering the touch of new crisp cotton. TJ gives you a blue mug of coffee and asks if you have found anywhere to live. You notice the two girls stop talking. So you say yes, moving into a flat next week; which might be true if social services sort things out. One of the girls sneaks a look at you and then whispers something to her friend. They giggle together, the tall one fiddling with the tiny gold earring in her right ear. When you look down, you see the tea stain on your jeans and the mud on your trainers. You are still wearing the old leather jacket that Nicola got from the Oxfam shop; the pelt still reeking of other lives that left their mark before your own imprint of tobacco and old car. Under the loud beat of the stereo, you can hear the girls giggle again. You grab your bag, out of the shop quick and back into the market square where the town hall clock strikes eleven o'clock and the rest of the day is a brick wall.

It's warm in the shopping arcade, heading for somewhere to sit, the two benches outside Boots are solid with old people and greasy grey hair. You keep walking past the shop windows already filled with Christmas glitter and wander into Dixon's to check the price of personal stereos. Your hand slides along the plastic covers in silver, blue, black as the price tickets laugh up at you. Then out past the bus station, down to the canal. There is no one else under the bridge yet, so you find a piece of dry cardboard and sit with your back against the red concave bricks of the bridge watching a Pepsi can floating in the water. Your bones are as cold as mud; you light up one of the cigarettes that Benji gave you last night and close your eyes. Traffic on the bridge above your head gives you a rhythm; your own words tumble round your head as you picture yourself on stage rapping . . .

> You're like a kid without a treat
> When you snivel to the beat
> There's a lump in your throat
> Because you've hit a low note
> Now you're down on the ground
> Hell, your dad is coming round.

The rap is falling into place when the voice of PC Harrap cracks open your rhythm with his usual threats that he can arrest you for vagrancy. You stand up to your full six feet two and look down at him, notice the dandruff on his navy jacket, and ask him how such a short-arse got into the force. As he takes out his notebook, you grab your bag and run.

You keep running until you find a bench in the park and slump down on to the green wooden planks that are tattooed with initials and love hearts. You remember last week at the youth centre when you sat next to Stacey and she talked to you for thirty-eight minutes. It was normal talk, about what music you both like and how she wants to train to be a nursery nurse because she loves kids. You heard yourself say that you want to be a car mechanic. Just once you looked at her face, while she smoked, and you saw her long eyelashes close over her blue-grey eyes as the smoke curled above her head. When she passed you the spliff you could taste her lips and you had to bend over and pretend to do up your laces so she couldn't see that you were getting hard. You move along on the bench hoping to find *Stacey 4 Liam* in the green cracked paint. Even you would be able to read that.

On the way to social services, Nicola explains who will be at the case conference. Your head is drumming as soon as you walk in the building and the stink of air freshener fails to hide any histories. The meeting room is so big that thirteen homeless people could live here. The faces around the table all stop talking as you take a chair next to Nicola. You recognise the Fat Bitch from benefits and Barry who is supposed to sort out your housing. There is a bloke in a suit you have never seen before and Kath the social worker. They talk and talk and talk. About you. As if you are not there. They use words you've never heard before. Your throat fills up with that lump again and the drumming in your head is nothing like Eminem. Fat Bitch tells everyone that your behaviour in the benefits office is unacceptable. Nicola says that they need to understand that you have difficulty filling in forms (polite words for stupid), that you are homeless (apart from the car), that you are only seventeen and your frustration is understandable. There is more talk and more words like homelessness legislation, children's act, duty of care, protocols, funding. As if you are not there.

Barry asks you where you are sleeping. You tell him nowhere. He says he can fix you up in a hostel in Newcastle. You hear Nicola's voice, 'Barry, he walked forty miles to get away from the smack-head scene there. The doctor said he and Benji had the nearest thing to trench foot he had ever seen. How could you suggest he goes back there?'

Something in your head breaks open and you are out of your chair. Fat Bitch looks scared. As you catch sight of yourself in the reflective glass in the door the devil is really grinning. And you know that this is the hell that you learned about in catechism class and this misery will last for eternal life. You have to get out, out, out. Your head is yammering and you are running up the road past people scurrying home in the rain. You crash against woollen shoulders, plastic bags of shopping and umbrella spokes. When you get to Queens Road you can see Benji's bike at number forty two.

You flop into the armchair, still panting from running through town. He makes you a coffee and gives you a smoke. Benji's room is a single bed, one armchair, a white plastic table, cupboard under a sink and the wooden wardrobe that still has the scar from Mack's last visit. The remnants of Benji's takeaway remind you that you've only eaten toast all day. You cannot move; just beginning to feel the heat of the coffee through the mug; lungs slowing down to normal speed; toes still nagging. When he asks about the meeting, you just shake your head. He tells you that one of the other bed-sits in the house will be free soon, Hazza is moving down south. You think about the last room you called your own and you remember your mother putting the new Manchester United duvet on the bed for your tenth birthday. In your plastic bag you find the Eminem CD and ask Benji if he can play it. The throb of the text fills your head. Your eyes close, '*Lose yourself in the music, the moment, the music, you own it . . .*'

Six months ago, you and Benji were walking from Newcastle together. You never knew why his parents kicked him out. He is real smart; now he has a job, a bike and a bed-sit, and is going to college at night. You are just plain dumb and sleep in the wreck of a car. By ten o'clock the room is full of smoke. Hazza is on the bed, Benji is on the floor by the stereo, you have not moved from the armchair. When you put your hand to your face, you feel another new spot on your forehead and the scratch of two days' growth on your chin. Neither Hazza nor Benji have money or a CD player you can borrow. You decide that first thing tomorrow you'll pawn your silver St. Christopher. Hazza passes round the spliff and Benji tells you that he has to chuck you all out before eleven o'clock or he could lose his tenancy.

At the door, Benji puts his hand on your shoulder and tells you it is payday tomorrow and he will meet you at the chip shop when he finishes work. You turn away to face the rain and keep your head down as you walk through the town. Your mouth is dry and your stomach is growling; you keep your eyes on the pavement and hope that Mack is not amongst the crowds coming out the pub. You focus on the rap you are writing in your head and the words that fall together.

> My heart is tapping in my ribcage
> Who wants this life at my age?
> Living in a car in a railway siding
> Wishing I was safe and not colliding
> With Mack and his mates or pervy Pete
> Just want to live in a place real neat.

When you get back to the car, the dope is wearing off and you don't know if your face is wet from rain or crying. Under the blanket, you welcome the familiar smell of plastic car seat and wonder if you will ever be warm again. Every noise is a nightmare keeping you awake. You think you can hear footsteps outside the car but you daren't look. Your hand sneaks out from the blanket and pushes down the button to lock the car door. It's the only thing in the car that still works. You pull your hood over your ears where your earphones should be.

Maybe it is the mixture of dope and skunk weed but you have a dream, or is it a visitation? Just when the future is all darkness and devil, you see the Virgin Mary standing beside you. She is the statue that towered above you at Catholic Mass each Sunday with your gran. The face is porcelain white and her veil is summer blue over long flowing cream robes. You feel her hand on your arm and a warm glow seems to flow through her fingers and around your whole body. She smiles and says, 'Everything will be fine.'

It has stopped raining when the first coal train wakes you. Inside, you feel the warmth of your dream. Outside is a metallic sky. When you go down to the fence for a piss you see a plastic Dixon's shopping bag on the ground amongst the drooping weeds. You pick it up, inside you see a shiny package. Back in the car there is just enough light from the railway for you to open the cardboard box. It's a brand new CD personal player. Perhaps you are dreaming but you get yourself plugged in and settle down under the early morning damp of the blanket. Eminem takes over, 'Lose yourself in the music, the moment, the music, you own it . . .'

After a couple of hours sleep, you get out of the car to a weak sun. Walking towards the youth centre, the new CD player keeps Eminem rapping in your head, you caress your arm which still feels the warm touch of the Virgin Mary. In the distance, PC Harrap strides the pavement.

VALE BENSON

Initiation at Graaff-Reinet

I<small>T IS</small> ten o'clock in the morning. My wife gone to work and I am sleeping in my bed when my cell phone ring.

It is David, my boss. He say, 'Isaac, man, you better get yourself down here right away. I got two tourists coming for township tour and they be here in twenty minutes.'

I had to make big rush. Splash water on face, get into tour-guide uniform, fast walk to town and David's office. No coffee, no nothing.

I thinking two people is not good for a township tour. I get R100 for each tour. Township tours take two hours, sometimes three. Eight, ten people in one trip is better, because of the tips. But now is end of season. Beginning of March is not a good time. January, February, March I earn almost nothing. No money.

So I stand in David's office in Graaff-Reinet main street. It is a nice, cool office. It is a shop, too. Sell big photograph books about South African wild life, South African plants and trees, South African tribes and local customs. Many white people buy them. Expensive books.

Then tourists come in. Two aunties. One auntie is a Boer with short hair and a voice for asking loud questions. The small auntie don't talk so much. She say she from Scotland. I don't know about no Scotland. She sound like she from England to me.

I say 'Good morning.'

Boer auntie say, 'Very nice to meet you. What is your name?'

I tell her, Isaac.

'Well, Isaac,' Boer auntie say. 'I really looking forward to this. I never done township tour before.'

English auntie who say she from Scotland ask me would I mind if she recorded my township tour talk on her little cassette machine. I say I am very happy if she do this.

We get in the minibus and go. Just outside the township I show them the field behind the High School and tell them this is where the young men go for initiation ceremony.

'Oh, really!' say Boer auntie in a big voice. 'I am very interested in these ceremonies. You must tell me all about them. I want to know about the male and the female initiation ceremonies.'

So I tell about the killing of the goats and I tell about some of the things the young men learn when they go to initiation camp.

'How long do they have to stay there?' Boer auntie asks.

I tell her, three weeks.

Boer auntie want to know more, so I tell her about the cutting, and about the burning of the clothes and belongings after the cutting.

I don't say nothing about female initiation and Boer auntie forgets to ask again, so we go into the township.

'Eleven to twelve thousand people live in this township,' I tell them.

Both aunties say, 'Really?' and look around.

'Yes,' I say. 'And these houses here are the newest, built by the new housing project of Mandela.'

Boer auntie say, 'Really?' again, and look at the houses.

English-say-she-from-Scotland-auntie just smiles and hold up her little recording machine.

'Are there enough houses for everyone?' Boer auntie ask me.

'No,' I say, 'but soon our government is building more houses here.'

Then I start to tell them about the schools we have on the township.

'Is the education free'? English auntie from Scotland want to know.

'No, it is not free,' I say. 'It cost R20 a month to send a child to pre-primary school, and R70 to send your child to primary school, and R100 a year for the high school. But some of these people are just lazy,' I tell the aunties. 'For one year now, our government give grant to families with no money. If they don't bother to get grants, their kids don't get no education.'

'Maybe they can't fill in the forms?' English-from-Scotland auntie say.

'We have councillors here do that for people who don't read or write,' I say.

She smiles and nods. 'Sometimes it takes a while for people to find out about these services,' she say.

I getting fed-up with this. 'Now we can go visit a pre-primary school,' I tell them.

We walk round the side of the school. The children are playing in the yard. Some of them come to the wire netting, waving and getting excited.

'Oh, this is wonderful,' say Boer auntie. 'I just love these children. They are the real future of South Africa, don't you think so, Isaac?'

I say yes, because, during the struggles, lots of black kids dropped out of school to get involved in the political action.

double meaning

Many of us hardly went to school at all. That is why we don't have proper jobs.

'These children are *so amazing*,' Boer auntie say. 'And the *most amazing* thing about them is that they don't notice colour at all. They just don't see it.'

I don't say nothing.

We go into the yard and some little kids run to say hello. One boy sit with some others but he howling and bawling.

'Why is that little boy crying?' English auntie from Scotland want to know.

I don't say nothing and go on walking to the school where the teachers have come out to tell the kids play time over.

'How many children come to this school?' Boer auntie asks.

I tell her one hundred and thirty, one hundred and forty.

'And how many teachers do they have here?'

I tell her, three.

'But that's one teacher to over forty children!' she say.

I don't say nothing.

Then English-from-Scotland auntie come carrying the kid who is crying. He clinging to her neck and she wiping his nose and speaking English to him.

I see the teachers not happy. 'He must just bumped his head,' one say. They take him from the auntie and put him in classroom. He cry louder.

'But *why* is he crying?' English-from-Scotland auntie ask again.

I look at her straight. 'You know,' I say, 'some of these children, they never seen white people before. This the first time. So they can be scared of white faces.'

English-from-Scotland auntie looks surprised. Then she say, 'Well, he let me pick him up. He wouldn't do that if he scared of me, would he?'

'You think?' I say.

Then we go into the schoolroom and the children all waiting to sing for the tourists. They sing many songs in English and Afrikaans and Xhoisa. They clap their hands and wave their arms in the air as they sing. The Boer auntie say, how amazing and how wonderful and they the future of South Africa. English-from-Scotland auntie just look like she going to cry.

Both aunties take lots of photographs.

Then I get the boss teacher, Mrs Mbatha, to show the aunties the store room and the kitchen and the rows of little toilets and washbasins. Aunties say these all lovely and sweet. Mrs Mbatha also tell about thief break-in at weekend. How he get in kitchen window and throw food around kitchen but only take CD player. Mrs Mbatha tell aunties CD player is new one, just bought with money sent by charity. Mrs Mbatha say thief been caught and is in police station jail right now. I say that is good.

When Mrs Mbatha leave room, I ask aunties to give something for the school. They get out their purses and I hear Boer auntie say to English-from-Scotland auntie that R100 between them will be enough.

Then aunties want photos in playground with kids sitting on their knees, and then they do lots of waving and saying goodbye, goodbye, and we get out of Tsolambo pre-primary school.

Outside the school, English-from-Scotland auntie point to one of the township lights.

'Is that where your electricity come from?' she asks.

I tell her we call them apartheid lights.

'Why is that?' Boer auntie asks.

'Because during the apartheid there have been the riots, the burning of the houses; many things go on, especially after Mandela was arrested,' I say. 'So the apartheid government decide to install these lights. So, even at night, the policemen could stay on that mountain behind us, and then they could see everything that is happening. They are like spotlights. If three, four people seen talking together in the street, then police would come down and arrest them.'

'Those were terrible times,' Boer auntie say. 'Now we must all work together to build up this country.'

I don't say nothing. I take them to the old town. Here all the houses are corrugated iron or wood. Falling apart. Streets just gravel and smelling of piss. We go into a shabeen. Aunties don't buy no drinks. Everybody in shabeen smiles and old Lily shakes aunties' hands and don't want to stop shaking them because she so drunk. Amos comes up. He shakes their hands too, and tells them he loves all tourists. He drunk as well.

Aunties smile and talk to Lily and Amos like they old friends, then they move away quick.

English auntie from Scotland say to me, 'I feel bit embarrassed, like we just looking at their poverty. Don't the people here mind tourists coming into the township?'

I tell her people in township very glad apartheid is over, very glad tourist come to townships, very happy to have their pictures taken.

I show them a row of very old shacks. I tell them it called Monarchy Street because all the men that live there fought for Britain in Second World War.

'They must be very old men now,' Boer auntie say.

'They not old now, they dead,' I tell her. 'Different people live in those shacks now.'

Then I show aunties where Robert Sobukwe was born. Start telling them about the Pan-African Congress and how Sobukwe the only black leader held as political prisoner during apartheid times.

'We know, we know!' Boer auntie say. 'We been to Robben Island. We done prison tour.'

Then Boer auntie ask English auntie from Scotland to take picture of her standing outside Sobukwe's house.

When they booked tour, aunties told my boss, David, they wanted to be taken to township restaurant and eat traditional African food. So I tell aunties we go for lunch now. They look very pleased. They not thin aunties.

I take them to only restaurant in township. It belonging to my friend, Nosphiwe. Aunties look around. 'Very nice,' they say.

I tell them how Nosphiwe got grant from government to start up restaurant.

While we wait for meal, Boer auntie start asking me questions again:

'Are you married, Isaac?'

I tell her, yes.

'And how many children do you have?'

I tell her God has not sent us children yet, but we hope.

'And do you come from Graaff-Reinet?'

I tell her, no, I come from Free State.

'Why you come to live in Graaff-Reinet, then?'

I tell Boer auntie that I meet my wife at Church Convention in Pretoria. My wife from Graaff-Reinet, so I come here to marry her.

'Oh, that very good,' say Boer auntie, and she laugh like it big joke. 'And tell me about your church, Isaac. What is it called? What do you believe in?'

I tell her that my church believe that God is important but ancestors are important too.

Boer auntie get very excited. 'This very interesting to me,' she say. 'I think you black cultures way ahead of us white cultures when it comes to recognising importance of ancestors. White people used to call the Sangomas "witch doctors" and say they the bad guys, but in recent years western cultures begin to understand effect ancestors have on all of us.' I don't know about white people's ancestors. I go into kitchen for word with Nosphiwe.

When I come back to aunties I tell them more about my church. How it started by my grandfather, how we ask ancestors for help, how we do ceremonies and how we do healing.

'This something I very interested in, Isaac,' say Boer auntie. 'I like to know more about it.'

I tell aunties they very welcome to come to my church tomorrow evening. Boer auntie say that would be very good and English auntie from Scotland say she like to come too.

I tell aunties they also able to meet my wife and my wife's mother tomorrow night as well. My wife's mother is healer-woman.

After aunties finish eating, Nosphiwe come in and sit with us. She have leather thong with animal hair on end of it and she waving thong as she ask aunties if they are well and if they enjoy township tour.

Boer auntie answer, 'We very well and we enjoy township tour very much, but what is that you are holding in your hands?'

Nosphiwe tell Boer auntie that it given to her by the Sangoma. It leather and hair from goat killed in ceremony. Nosphiwe also say that she had calling to be a Sangoma.

'How do you know when you have a calling?' Boer auntie asks.

Nosphiwe tell her it when you have same dream over and over again. That dream is a message from the ancestors.

'And have you started your Sangoma training?'

Nosphiwe tell her, not yet, but soon.

'And where will you go for your training?'

Nosphiwe say she will go to Sangoma school.

'And where is that?' Boer auntie want to know.

All this time English-from-Scotland auntie say nothing, but she sit and press buttons on her little tape recorder.

I think this is enough. 'I am sorry, but we must leave now,' I say. 'David is waiting for me at office.'

Then aunties make big hurry, grabbing their cameras for last photos. Boer auntie has one taken with Nosphiwe. Boer auntie puts arm round Nosphiwe like they sisters. Then Boer auntie has picture taken standing with me like I her brother.

When we say goodbye, aunties tell me what a wonderful time they have and how much they enjoy township tour. 'And we see you tomorrow at your church,' they say. 'We looking forward very much to visiting your church and meeting your family.'

I give Boer auntie my cell phone number. Then I go home and tell my wife that tomorrow the aunties come to our house. I tell my mother-in-law what she must do to be ready for aunties.

I am very happy and I wait for Boer auntie to phone me.

No phone call comes. Aunties don't visit my church. I never hear from those aunties again.

HELEN DUNMORE

With Shackleton

A THUD, a squeal, a pair of hot, tight arms around her neck.

'It snowed! There's millions of snow in the garden!'

Clara pulls away, rushes to the window and begins to drag at the heavy curtains.

'No, Clara, be careful! Wait a minute –'

Isabel slides out of bed. And there it is, the snow lighting the dark garden, heaped on the window ledges. A blackbird flies out of the laurels, breaking loose a shower of snow. There's not a footprint on the white lawn.

Clara is silent too. How far away last winter must seem to her. It snowed then, and Stephen took her up to the Heath on the sledge. Clara was only five, muffled in scarf and woollen helmet. Isabel had even wound a shawl around Clara's legs. The child couldn't stir.

The sledge's runners stuck in the fresh snow. Stephen tugged on the rope, the sledge broke free with a jerk, and away they went, Stephen loping ahead, the sledge bounding behind.

Isabel was wearing her new red kimono, with her coat thrown on top. There'd been no question of her going with them that day. She'd watched them out of sight, and then gone back indoors, sleepy again, yawning as she climbed the stairs. She held on to the banisters. Stephen was always telling her to take more care. He liked to think of her as impulsive, skimming over the surface of life. Perhaps it's the things we believe about people that make up their charm for us, thinks Isabel. What if Stephen knew the heavy knot of fears that lay coiled inside her?

She'd dormoused by her bedroom fire all morning. Such delicious, luxurious, justified sleepiness. Mrs Elton had brought up her cocoa at eleven. Isabel loathed cocoa as a rule, but all through that winter she craved it. Thick, delicious cocoa, made with the top of the milk. And again, usually Isabel was embarrassed to be found on her little bedroom sofa, doing nothing. But it was all right, on that particular day, and on all those days last winter. Mrs Elton put the cocoa down and announced, 'There's a good half-pint of best morning milk in there. And a boy's just this minute come to clear the steps. I'll put some ashes down once he's done, and then you'll be safe to go out. It looks as if this freeze is going to hold.'

'Wonderful cocoa,' Isabel breathed, not because she felt she had to, but because it was true.

'There's nothing like milk to build good bones,' said Mrs Elton, folding her arms and looking down at Isabel as if Isabel belonged to her. And they were off. They couldn't help it. The irresistible topic swam into view – as if it were ever out of view! – and in they plunged after it.

Isabel had bathed in approval, day after day. She could lie on that sofa for the entire nine months if she felt like it, and there wouldn't be a murmur. Not even from that she-elephant, Stephen's mother. Isabel had done what was wanted of her. Her mother-in-law had 'spoken her mind quite openly', once Clara turned four. Stephen had always wanted a large family. The Kendalls ran to large families. And naturally Stephen wanted a son to bear his name. Any man would. The fact that he didn't talk about it meant absolutely nothing. Stephen was far too considerate, but Josephine believed in frankness.

'In fact,' said Josephine Kendall, 'I don't really regard it as a family, if there is only one child.'

A stain of red touched Isabel's cheeks. Not a family! Perhaps one day a manhole would be left uncovered and Josephine Kendall would step on to nothing with her usual splendid self-assurance, and plunge fathoms deep into the sewers of London.

But at the same time Isabel could not help longing for her mother-in-law's approval. She knew it was weak, the kind of self-betrayal that made her twist angrily in her bed at night. If she'd had someone of her own, it might have been different. Isabel's mother was dead.

'And do you know, my dear, she hasn't even managed to keep her own mother alive . . .' Isabel could just imagine those words, uttered in the trumpeting half-whisper that her mother-in-law employed with the little crowd of evil-minded old monuments who were her intimate friends. Old monuments all of them, old she-elephants trampling and trumpeting and blundering their way through the jungle of north London. And Josephine Kendall, with her hanging flaps of jowl and her massive ankles, was the oldest, most obstinate and deadly elephant of them all.

Isabel had no one of her own, except for Stephen, and now Clara. Her father lived in Brussels – 'a most peculiar place to choose, and nobody knows quite what he lives on,' trumpetted the elephants – and as for her brother, none of the Kendalls counted him.

But Stephen counts Rod, thinks Isabel quickly. Stephen likes Rod.

Clara breaks away from the snowy window, and begins

to stamp up and down the bedroom carpet, her face pale with excitement.

'Can we go out now? Can we go out now this minute?'

Isabel takes a deep breath. 'Yes,' she says. Clara swings round and stares at her mother sternly, searching her face. Isabel knows what she's waiting for: the usual adult excuses, qualifications: After you've had your breakfast, when we've tidied up all the toys, when your cold's better . . .

'Yes,' she repeats, 'now, this minute. We'll just throw on our clothes, and go.'

Clara's face creases with delight. 'Throw on our clothes!' she cackles.

Isabel catches the excitement. She'll do just exactly that. No bath, no brushing and twisting and pinning of her hair, no patting cream into her skin. Why she keeps on with it all anyway, God knows, since Stephen's not here. And won't be for –

Don't think of that. She crams on an old tweed skirt, a woollen jumper, her thickest stockings.

'Now let's get you ready. But hush, we don't want to wake Louie.' They creep into the nursery. Louie is still asleep in the adjoining room. She should be up by now. But what is Louie, after all? Just about seventeen, and still growing, judging from the way her wrists poke out her sleeves. How Isabel used to sleep when she was seventeen, as if sleep were food.

Clara is utterly silent as Isabel fishes in the chest of drawers, finding knitted leggings, woollen skirt and jersey. Clara's outdoor things are downstairs: good.

'Aren't you going to wash me?' whispers Clara hoarsely.

'Not this morning. Ssh.'

'You go to hell if you don't wash.' Clara doesn't sound

troubled by the prospect, but all the same Isabel whispers back, 'That's nonsense. All that happens if you don't wash is that you smell like an old cheese.'

Clara convulses with silent laughter. Isabel grabs the clothes, lifts Clara and hurries downstairs.

'You don't have to carry me, I'm not a baby,' Clara hisses in her ear, drumming hard little heels on Isabel's hips.

The sledge, Isabel knows, is hanging on a nail in the garden shed. She tells Clara to wait at the door, and sets off across the snowy waste of the lawn. The light is so strong that she blinks.

'Here we are, Clara, you sit down here, and I'll pull you with the rope.'

'And then I'll pull you, Mummy.'

'I'm too heavy for you.'

But the truth is that she has lost weight, pounds and pounds of it. She is thin now. Her old tweed skirt sags at the waist, and her face is pinched.

'Poor Isabel, she's lost her bloom,' she heard the elephants say one day, as they popped little egg-and-cress triangles into their mouths with their trunks. All the great grey ears flapped in agreement.

Isabel begins to drag the sledge uphill. It is surprisingly heavy. She turns round, but of course there is only Clara on the sledge. How could there be anyone else?

Josephine Kendall believes that it is high time Isabel pulled herself together. After all, everyone has had a miscarriage. Why, she herself . . .! Even a late miscarriage, although of course not very nice, is something that you must not allow yourself to dwell on. You simply have to pick yourself up and try again.

The other elephants nodded again, although perhaps a shade less certainly than before.

The pavement has already been trodden. Milkmen and postmen and bakers' boys have been out already, she supposes. Her breath steams. A woman in a grey wrapper is scattering ash on the steps of a raw brick house that seems too tall for itself.

'Clara, can you get off and walk this bit?'

Clara looks sternly at her mother. 'Daddy pulled me all the way up this hill.'

So she does remember.

'Is Daddy pulling a sledge now?'

'No. You remember, I told you. Their sledges are much bigger than this, and they are pulled by dogs.'

'Dogs like Bella?'

'Bella's far too small. Remember what Daddy told you about the dogs?' A frown almost settles on Clara's face.

'I don't remember what he said. I don't even remember what his face looks like.'

'You do, Clara. Just close your eyes and you'll see it.'

'No,' says Clara, shaking her head like a judge, 'I don't not even remember what his tongue looks like. I'm afraid it's gone,' she adds. The sound of one of Josephine's favourite phrases on her daughter's lips makes Isabel want to slap Clara. False self-deprecation followed by deadly insult: how typical of Josephine it was. 'I know I ought to remember your name, but I'm afraid it's gone.'

'They are called huskie dogs,' she says levelly. 'And stop kicking snow into your boots, Clara.'

She takes Clara's hand and they walk on, the sledge dragging behind them. Close your eyes and you'll see it. But no, she realises, it's not as easy as that. She can capture the back of Stephen's head perfectly, but his face is turned away. She gives Clara's hand a little squeeze.

'Sorry I was cross, Clarrie.'

But Clara answers out of quite a different train of thought.

'Are they biting dogs, where Daddy is?'

'No. They don't bite people. Only their food.'

'What is their food?'

'Oh – meat.'

'Is that Daddy's food too?'

'Yes, but he has other things as well.'

'What other things?'

'Things out of tins, and biscuits.'

'And things from the Stores.'

'There isn't any Stores there. You remember the pictures we showed you.'

'Actually they are building a Stores where Daddy is,' says Clara casually. 'I saw it in the newspaper. Anyway my feet are cold.'

'Come here, let me rub them.'

She pulls Clara's right foot out of its boot, and brushes off the snow. Her leggings are not too damp. Isabel takes off her own gloves and chafes the foot with her bare hands.

'Are you really cold, Clara? Do you want to go home?'

'We haven't even gone down a hill yet!' Tears of exasperation jump to Clara's eyes.

'All right, sit on the sledge again, and I'm going to wrap my big scarf round your feet, like this.'

As for where Stephen is, she's not even going to think about it. Josephine had been bursting with it when the invitation came, her trunk pointing to heaven as she trumpeted the news around her circle. Stephen, Isabel's gentle, funny, thoughtful Stephen, was going off to some unimaginable wasteland of howling winds and blistering cold, to spend weeks and weeks struggling to reach a place that wasn't even a place at all. Just a point on the compass. Josephine could scarcely have been more thrilled if she'd managed to send Stephen into battle.

'A most remarkable opportunity. He simply leapt at it. The Society –'

How many Stephens were there? There was her Stephen, so close that she couldn't describe him. Gentle, funny, thoughtful: yes, he was all those things, sometimes more, sometimes less, but they weren't really what he was. She could not add up Stephen in words. The closer people came, perhaps the less they saw each other. Like bringing something so close to your eyes that it went out of focus.

But Josephine's Stephen was quite another matter.

'I feel I must give you a word of warning, Isabel dear, at such a very exciting time for us all. You do realise that it can cause great trouble in a marriage if a man is not allowed to pursue his career because of all sorts of fearfulness and tearfulness – and of course to be invited to take part was the most extraordinary honour – although naturally no more than we know Stephen deserves – I happen to know that Archie Cannington himself recommended Stephen most highly – You know who I'm talking about, Isabel dear? I only speak to you like this because your own mother –'

'Not allowed?'

'Come, Isabel, you know what I mean. A man must feel that his wife is behind him.'

Maybe that's why I can only see the back of his head, thinks Isabel now, because I am behind him.

At last, at last she has dragged Clara up to the top of the

hill. Her heart thumps, and she is sweating. She must get strong again, she must. She will drink a glass of milk every morning if it chokes her, and eat second helps of everything, as Rod used to say. When summer comes, she'll go down to Eastbourne for sea bathing. She glances behind her. Clara is sitting tight on the sledge, her mittened hands gripping its sides. She beams at her mother. There is not the smallest cloud of doubt in the sky of Clara's face.

And now they are up there, on top. The white vista spreads. There's the city, smoking in the cold, remote and intricate as a jewel. Ants of people toil up the slopes with sledges and tin trays.

But would he have gone anyway, even if the baby had been born? His little boy, seven months old by now, bundled in shawls and peeping at a white world for the first time. Isabel would not have failed, and Stephen would have shut the door on his adventure. He'd have done it reluctantly – she had to admit that – but he would have done so. Even the most fearsome rampages and trumpeting of all the she-elephants in north London could not have influenced him.

'Mummy! Mummy! I want to slide down the hill.'

Suddenly the hill looks very steep. Has she come to the right part of the Heath? Is this the place where Stephen brought Clara? Perhaps it isn't safe. If they run over a bump and Clara is thrown off and she strikes her head against a stone concealed by the snow –

'Mummy! I'm getting cold again.'

'All right. Hold tight to the rope now, Clara, while I get on.'

Isabel places the child between her legs, tucking up the folds of her skirt. The runners of the sledge fidget on the snow. The sledge wants to trick her by sliding forward slowly, inch by inch until it's got the momentum it wants and it can swoosh forward, catching her off-balance so she loses hold of the rope and then –

But it's not going to happen, not until she's ready. She digs her heels in, takes the rope from Clara and then eases the sledge forward, under control. They are at the lip of the hill.

'Hold tight, Clara.'

Clara grips her mother's knees. Isabel shoves off. The sledge sticks. She pushes harder and suddenly the sledge shoots forward, over the edge. She gasps as the cold air flies past her. A bump in the ground jolts the sledge and then they are gathering speed, hissing down the fresh, clean icy snow with the rope taut in Isabel's hands. And for a moment Isabel is superb, steering them masterfully to the left of a bush while Clara screams with pleasure.

The slope slackens. The sledge runs out, losing speed, and comes to rest in a deep, unsullied patch of snow. Isabel clambers off.

'I didn't remember it was like that,' says Clara. Her cheeks flare like poppies. 'Is that what Daddy's doing?'

'You mean now this minute?'

'Yes.'

'I'm not sure.'

Those cliffs and lakes of ice, those deep crevasses shining blue, those winds so cold they burn like fire. Is that where Stephen is? She can't get close to him. She can't hear what he is saying, or listen to his breathing. He is much too far away. Just a dot, like a baby before it's grown or born. Come back, she begs him. Come closer. But even when she manages to bring him back into focus, all he does is to hammer pegs into the ground and fix twine between them, before taking careful measurements.

'I want to do it again,' says Clara. Isabel looks at her. Clara sounds so exactly like Josephine that Isabel almost expects to see her daughter swing a tender, baby trunk. But she also sounds so like Stephen that Isabel's eyes prickle.

'You're sure you'll be all right, Isabel? Because if you minded dreadfully, you know, I wouldn't –'

'I want to do it again. Are you listening, Mummy? I want to do it again.'

'All right, but help me pull the sledge back up the hill.'

The child takes the rope in her fist. Isabel holds it too, and they begin to haul the sledge up the steep slope. Isabel is soon out of breath.

'Let's stop a minute, Clara.'

'Are you tired?' demands Clara, her face suddenly tense. She shouldn't look like that, thinks Isabel.

'No,' she replies, 'Not tired a bit. We'll get our breath, and then we'll go on up.'

Clara searches her mother's face with bright, suspicious eyes. She doesn't trust me, thinks Isabel. She doesn't think I'm strong enough. I've cried in front of her. Weak, oozing tears that slipped out, hour after hour. Clara stared, then put on a bright blank face and ran off to find Louie.

What does she think about Stephen being gone? What does she really think? The elephants have told her how proud she must be. Isabel has told her that Stephen thinks of Clara every night, before she goes to sleep. But they are all lying, thinks Isabel. And she herself, why she's the greatest liar of them all. Her 'gentle, funny, thoughtful Stephen'. Why does she tell herself such stuff? Why does she want to edit Stephen so ruthlessly?

He explained it all to her. The clothing he would wear, the instruments they were taking, the pack ice, the way the ship was designed to yield to the pressure of the ice rather than be crushed. He told her about sea leopards, of whose existence she had never suspected. So many things, a jumble of them spilling out on to the carpet as he stood with one foot on the fender, his eyes alight with unshared joy.

He was pregnant with his journey. She didn't understand that then, but now she does. The journey was all folded away inside him, a life that was as real and immediate as his own heartbeat, but to everyone else just a possibility that might happen or might not happen. And if it didn't happen, well, it was not a tragedy. Pick yourself up and start all over again.

For him, it has happened. He is there. He isn't thinking of her or of Clara, she knows it in her bones. She doesn't expect him to do so. He's taking measurements, skilfully and meticulously, to make a map where previously there has not been a map. It is summer there, or what they call summer. At the end of his long day he'll lie in his sleeping bag, writing up notes.

She was happy to let them go off together that day last winter, without her. She wasn't fearful, because she had her own baby safe inside her. Such calm is a kind of folly, she thinks now. It's self-deception.

'Don't take your mittens off, Clara.'

'My hands are sweating so much they are wet,' says Clara, with her usual severe accuracy. She has pulled off both mittens. She wriggles the fingers of her left hand, and spreads them out into the shape of a star. Impossible to believe that hand was ever part of Isabel's own body. Clara is so separate, so forceful. She seizes the rope again.

'I want to pull it.'

'All right, see if you can.'

'Don't help me, Mummy, I want to do it all by my own.'

Clara starts to clamber up the steep side of the hill, hauling the sledge. She'll defy me all her life, thinks Isabel. It makes her want to laugh. And if the baby – yes, you're going to say it this time, she tells herself – if the baby had been born, he would have defied you too.

Stephen was sorry not to have his son. He'd looked at her with his eyes wide, bright, blank. 'I'm awfully sorry, Is.' Sorry for her, he meant. And she'd taken it as no more than her due.

There's that small dot again, far away in the wasteland of snow. He's bending over something, concentrated. She can't see his face, but she knows it will be taxed with thought. He has got to get this right. In the glassy, untrodden waste there is not so much as a single elephant's footprint to distract him.

'Look at me! Look at me, Mummy! I'm right up at the top of the world.'

And so she is. 'That's wonderful, Clara!' But Clara scorns her mother's hyperbole.

'Watch out!' she trumpets, 'I'm coming down!'

'Wait, Clara, not on your own –'

But the next minute Isabel has to leap aside as the sledge, propelled by a flushed and shrieking Clara, hurtles towards her. It careers on and overturns, depositing Clara in the snow. Clara gets to her feet in silence.

'Are you all right?'

'I meant that to happen,' says Clara. 'It's your turn now.'

Up the hill again. Suddenly Stephen is close. He's stopped for a breather, he's wiping his face and peering in her direction. But perhaps he doesn't even know that she is there. She won't distract him. With that sort of close, meticulous work, one slip can lose you hours.

When I was having Clara, she remembers, I didn't want Stephen in the room.

But all the same, almost in spite of herself, her hand creeps up. She gives a small, tentative wave. Does he see her, or not see her? It doesn't matter.

'I can't tell you, Is, what a feeling there is among the men.' No, she thought. You can't tell me. She shrank from his euphoria as if it were a flame that might burn her. He was so considerate, too. He left behind a thick packet of directions, to be opened 'in the eventuality of my death'. And he told the she-elephant of the packet's existence, but not Isabel. Josephine could not resist one fatal hint, and Isabel was on to it like a tiger.

They saw Isabel at last, those elephants of north London.

Here they are again, at the top of the hill. Here is Clara, taking the ropes. Isabel holds the sledge, steadying it.

'Ready, Clara?'

She pushes the sledge and it reaches the lip of the hill. It hesitates, then glides forward, gathering speed.

Here is her daughter, flying away from her. Stephen, from the bottom of the world, shades his eyes to see Clara fly.

ALEXANDRA FOX

Rounding the Corner

YOU'RE SITTING on the hard edge of your son's bed, smiling. You test the smile against your teeth, make sure it's firm. His wrist is hot, dry under your fingertips; you're counting his stuttering pulse against a half-minute sweep of the second hand. The watch ticks round, and it's like there's a counterpoint between your eyes and your fingers, with the rhythm of the beats never coinciding. You double it in your head, carry on for the whole minute to be sure, write it down.

Outside the boy-blue room the sky is low, whitewashed with broad strokes, the sort of day that was snow-weighted in your childhood. Now it's dull, cold, perhaps a spit of dirty rain. That's good. If it were snowing on the hill he'd see other children rolling, pelting, sledging, trudging, long to join them. It's snug in here as the afternoon light ebbs.

A heron flies past, neck stretched, forcing itself up over the ground with slow, heavy wingbeats.

'Mum?'

'Sorry. I was miles away.' You whip the thermometer from his mouth, glance at the digits, look again, and beep the button quickly, blanking the screen. You mark it on the chart, join the lines up, up.

'Mum . . . It's this goldfish thing . . . I just don't . . . understand . . . If a goldfish can't remember things, why does it matter if it's in a round bowl? When it comes round to where it was it won't remember where it started anyway.' He's very breathless today, a quick whispy gasp between each couple of words, his mouth blue-grey by the end of the sentence.

'That's just what I've been told, Timmy. They get bored going round in circles. And the square walls give them more oxygen, make it easier for them to breathe. It's kinder to put them in a tank with straight sides.'

'Can we get it tomorrow, anyway?'

'We'll see.'

Suddenly, Tim's eyes drop closed. His face is still, greasily dry like a white wax candle, but behind the blue of his eyelids his eyes twitch with life, and deep inside you feel a very first answering flicker of movement. Your hand moves, shields your belly. Guilt rises like acid in your throat.

At that moment your pager vibrates.

Somewhere in Europe a child has died or lies dying. You see in your mind a small boy's body, head and legs crushed bloody by the wheels of a car, the torso in between perfect, untouched. Or you see the explosion of an aneurism juicing a brain as a heart beats on in a mindless body, a little girl's face, golden ringlets, empty eyes.

And you think, why couldn't it have happened yesterday, last week . . . when Tim's temperature was only thirty-seven degrees, when his lungs weren't protesting with pain at every weakening breath, when he could still stand? Yet you know that you would cut parts off yourself with a rusty knife and relish the pain if it would give him more time – a finger for a day, an arm for a month, your heart for his lifetime. And you think of those other parents, without even that small hope, and feel sick.

You go downstairs to make the phone call. Mr Jadhav

tells you yes, that it's the best chance yet, a good size, a tight match, should be available in the morning. Come in now for a full work-up; you know what to bring with you. And you say nothing about the temperature up two degrees and climbing, the deep productive wheeze. You clench that knowledge deep inside you (with the flickering entity), and will it to go away.

There's an Arsenal holdall packed ready, hanging on a special hook in the corner of the hall. The car's full of fuel, as it's been since Tim's name climbed to the top of the list, nine long months ago, waiting. It's like an almost-term pregnancy, ready to go into labour at any moment, eager for the baby . . . the baby.

And the goldfish?

Tim's never had a pet; it's always been too risky. Eleven years of being careful, guarding that frail frame against allergic reactions. He's got books stacked under his bed like a teenager's dirty magazines, *How to Care for Your New Kitten*, *Choosing a Puppy*, *Rabbits and Guinea Pigs*.

'Have a heart,' he said to you (it was a private joke, and good that he could laugh about it). 'I'm taking all this stuff to fight infections. Can't I even have a hamster?'

You compromised on a goldfish, brought in the laptop, and spent a morning snuggled on the bed, trawling the net for breeds of cold-water fish and how to care for them. Malcolm said he'd buy the tank and gravel on the way home from work. You'd planned to set it up tonight, let Tim boss you both around so you did it properly, by the book, leaving it to settle for twenty-four hours so the chemicals could dissipate and the temperature regulate before you put the fish in. Now you don't know what to do.

'Timmy.'

He snaps awake instantly. 'Mum. Remember . . . it says it's got to be four litres capacity. Does Dad know that? And he's getting some weed – *cabomba* – and snails?'

'Timmy. I've just spoken to Mr Jadhav. We've got to go in now.'

'I know. I heard you . . . talking downstairs. They've got a good one?'

'Yes. But don't get too excited. Remember last time.'

'Yeah. But last time the heart was wrong. This time it's me, isn't it?'

'What do you mean?'

'I've not . . . been feeling right. My chest's kinda bouncy and it gurgles. It hurts. And when you've taken my temp you haven't shown it to me, and said look at that, Timmy, aren't you doing well.'

'Well, what shall we do about this fish? Shall we take it into the hospital? We could set it up in the day-room. Something to look forward to. Afterwards.'

'Okay.'

You put a hand behind the bony wings of his shoulders and help him pull on a sweatshirt, joggers. He smells sour, hot yet shivering. Tim drops his feet over the side of the bed and tries to stand. He sways, crumples. You wrap him in his Arsenal duvet and half-carry him down the stairs like a stumbling parcel, light, so very light.

'I am so sorry, Mrs Westbury, Anne. You must realise how sick he is.' The consultant has his arms folded. He looks down at himself, unfolds them, almost holds his hands out to you, but draws them back. His eyes are dark, nearly black, unreadable, unreachable.

'But we're so nearly there . . . after all these months.'

'He has grown too weak. His body cannot take the strain

of the operation. It is no longer only his heart that is in failure. We must not risk it.'

'Risk? What's to risk? He's dying. He can't even stand, for God's sake.'

'There are so few hearts, so much need. We have to give it to someone with a good statistical chance of longer-term survival. I am so very sorry. It is good that you brought Timothy into the hospital. He is very weak now. We will put him into the end room. He will have more peace in there.'

'There's nothing I can say to make you change your mind . . . to give us any hope at all? You can't just give up on him. He's a boy, only a boy . . . Mr Jadhav, I know you've got sons . . .' Your throat is wet, full. You need to spit the words out before the sobs take over so that you dissolve, seep. 'The room at the end. I see. Thank you.'

The room at the end of the corridor has walls of two-tone beige, Thunderbirds curtains washed into bruise-blue splodges, a reclining chair for the long watches of the night. It is quiet, apart.

You've dressed Tim in pyjamas from his ready-bag, blue, with a football embroidered on the pocket. They button loosely across his chest, but the legs flap a good inch above his ankles. His feet stick out, long almost-man feet with soft, straight toes, perfectly pink. You hate those extra inches of leg. Why was all that strength put into growing when it was needed for keeping strong? What do two inches of height matter, if he never becomes a man?

'They ought to put my name on here,' he says. 'A sticker on the bed-head saying Tim Westbury was here.'

Your own heart clenches. A shiver runs through you. You see a bench in a park, a brass plaque, 'In loving memory of

Timothy Westbury, Deacon of this Parish'. There's a goose walking over his granddad's grave.

You place his special photo on the locker, a little boy in a man-size football shirt, walking on to the pitch with his beloved Arsenal team, Timmy the mascot in an oxygen mask, cylinder dragging behind him like a dog on a lead, eyes alight with the wonder of life.

The soft-eyed young nurse knows Tim, but there's no teasing today. He tries to blow into the peak-flow meter for her; the pointer hardly moves. She takes blood and urine for testing. You draw his sleeve back down over his arm. He's hot enough already, but it's something to do and your hands are so useless, impotent. His eyes close and you sit, drinking him in. Hating, waiting.

You think of other tests, of the wand turning blue, wet with your own urine stream, of that sick guilt that flooded through you as you realised.

How could you have let it happen? Tim was coughing endlessly through the early hours one morning, and you stirred, moved to go to him. Malcolm put his hand out to hold you back, whispering, 'Anne . . . leave him, he's asleep, it won't do any good,' but his hand missed your shoulder, landed on your breast, and you'd forgotten the hugeness of its comfort, the way you fitted into it. He turned you to him, and you welcomed the dry soreness of him inside you, that pleasure-pain against the rhythm of Tim's dry, tearing cough, the pounding against you, until you wanted, needed more and strove with him, and the tears ran back into your ears, soaking your hair. Why would you even think of new life, nameless tissue fastening itself on to your womb, feeding, when life was being coughed away on the other side of the bedroom wall?

How can you let your cheeks bloom now, your belly swell, as Timmy hollows, fades?

Malcolm helps you set the fish tank up on a trolley. Tim's on a drip now, blue lines travelling up his arm. His mouth is set, white, and he's biting his lip, occasionally whimpering. He tries to pull the mask from his mouth. It's like a bee-sting, he says, but it's drilling into him. How long, Mum, how much longer? You comb his salt-stiff hair with your fingertips, through and through until it turns to silky locks between your fingers and your hands are soaked with that peardrop essence of fever and hospitals. Why do they put him through this pain? How long?

You don't know. You think about the fish.

So you tip multicoloured gravel into the bottom of the shiny new tank, spread it out, raking with your hands until it's smooth. You say to Tim, 'What about a hill in one corner, like the one at the park?' and he sort of nods but it could be a shake of the head. You build one anyway, set a 'No Fishing' sign on top, burrow with your fingers to plant drooping strands of weed.

Then you pour in fresh water, eight jugs of it, each half a litre, because the tank's just as big as Tim wanted. It's good the jug's so small because every time you fill it you have to walk along the scuffed corridor to the Ladies, turn the tap, wait, walk all the way back, slowly so it doesn't spill. If you had to stay in that room where agony is being squeezed from a plastic bag into your son's arm you don't think you could bear it, you'd rip the tubes out, and take him home, hold him tight, let him go.

The fish is called a Celestial. It's got protruding eyes, horribly ugly, the delight of a small boy's heart. He calls it Bugs. You shouldn't really put it into the tank yet. It should take time to become acclimatised, but Timmy wants, needs to see it swimming, so you do.

Night. You're curled in the recliner, no place for your head to rest except cricked on your shoulder, and your legs twitch restlessly. It isn't ever dark enough, but the sleepless discomfort feels right.

You might be having a nightmare.

You'd never thought of it before. There's a problem with a fish in a square-sided aquarium. It's the darkness on the outside, making the glass into a mirror. Tim's lying there, watching Bugs, but Bugs can't see him. Bugs just sees another Bugs in front of him, invading his space, reflected. He attacks, battering his head against the side.

Tim doesn't turn his head away. He's watching his fish bash, crash, thud its head against the side of the tank, again, again, smashing that bulging eye from its socket until it's floating from a thread. He doesn't scream.

'Mum,' he says in the morning, but he says it in single words. He's lying flat, skin grey-white as the winter sky. 'A round bowl's better. He'd be bored . . . but he wouldn't hurt himself.'

'Don't talk, Timmy. Rest.'

'Put him in a round bowl. He'll forget the other fish, forget he hurt himself. Mum . . . Mum.'

'Rest. Don't upset yourself. I'll move the tank back into the dayroom.'

Malcolm brings in a glass dish that evening. They don't seem to make round fishbowls any more. This one is a decorative vase, crystal clear. You scatter jewels of wet gravel in the bottom, transfer the water in your little jug, set down a tiny padlocked treasure chest, plant a tree of water weed in the middle with its fruit of tight clinging snails.

Malcolm wheels the trolley into the corridor while he moves the fish to his new home. He tucks a twitching plastic bag into his jacket pocket. He sits beside you on the bed and his hand seeks yours blindly, holds it hard.

'Timmy, see. He's happy in the new bowl. Look. Even his eye's got better. He isn't fighting any more.'

'Mum.'

'Yes, Timmy?' You lean close to his mouth. His voice is small.

'No. Don't let him . . .'

'What?'

'Don't throw Bugs . . . away . . . don't forget him . . . just cos he's hurt. . . . not fair. . . .'

'No, my darling. Of course we won't.'

And Malcolm slides the bag from his pocket, unfolds it. Bugs is quivering, gasping in the air, still alive, dripping. He tumbles into the water with a splash, his ghastly eye trailing behind him.

You sit on the edge of his bed, hold your son's wrist in your hand, smoothing the blue veins with your thumb, so softly. Malcolm strokes his hair the wrong way, rough stuff, dad stuff, loving stuff.

'Look, Timmy.'

He doesn't move.

You think he opens his eyes. They'll tell you that he didn't, but you know. There is surely a flicker, a little slit of an opening eye, an awakening just once more as Tim looks into the crystal bowl and sees the old fish and the new, swimming round together, forgetting.

JESSICA BOWMAN

Don't Know A Good Thing

'YOU SEE, Patricia,' her mother had said. 'See the rows all lined up like that? Nice and neat. Don't you let a seed get out of line, now. Keep them straight. See how nice it looks? Perfect. Long as you take care of them weeds, you won't have no problems.'

Trish had lived in Nupiak all her life. The small cabin with the added-on indoor toilet and lean-to firewood shed had been her childhood home – passed on from her grandmother, her mother, and when both were dead, to her. She was a quiet child, the only one left after the harsh winter of '76, when her older brother had succumbed to the flu in a frigid, blizzarding April. Trish had just turned ten. She stayed close to her mother ever since. When she was a little girl, the wind used to freeze her wet hair into black icicles if she went outside to help her mother in the garden after a bath. The year of the blizzard she had to break it off and wear it short because it was so cold; after that, she always dried it all the way through.

'Look at that,' her mother would sniff, wiping a strand of coarse black hair from her forehead. 'Just filth, that is.' Trish looked over at her neighbour's lot behind the house. The Shaws lived about a hundred yards away, but she could see their ramshackle place clearly in the early morning light. The garden was a mess – choked with fireweed and thick, foul-smelling clumps of red forest berries that were slowly overtaking the chain link; a rusted Chevrolet propped on cement blocks with a sagging roof collecting rainwater and melted snow.

'Filth,' her mother would shake her head and sniff again. 'All that space out here, all that land. Just don't know a good thing when they got it, them Shaws.'

After her mother died, Trish hosed the garden down one night and left it to freeze. The next day she broke off all the frigid stems above ground and let the cold earth alone until spring, when she tilled the ground and planted a garden of her very own to see if she could do it.

Trish first met Adlet during a blizzard. There was only the one bar in Nupiak, where all the men passed the time when they came through the village on floatplanes or fishing boats. She had come to deliver leeks to Sila when it struck, and they'd been holed up for five hours until the ploughs made it through and the wind died down.

Adlet had stopped for a drink with his fishing buddies after they'd flown in from Homer for the weekend. He ran a small shuttling service between villages. Sila introduced Trish and said, 'This lady here's the best damn green thumb this side of the Mother Nature, gentleman.' Trish blushed and the men laughed. Adlet, though, looked at her, cocking his head, and asked if she'd ever grown delphiniums. Trish nodded, secretly pleased. Delphiniums were her favourite.

'My mother grew delphiniums in Nome,' he said. 'I was always amazed they came back every year like that.'

'Yeah, well,' said Sila, 'you want to last a winter in the bush, you hang around Trish. She can make anything grow out here.'

*   *   *

130

Trish was pretty enough, with dark eyes like almonds, a pleasant roundish face, and long, inky black hair. Though Adlet wasn't the first man ever to buy her a drink, he was the first to see her stick around long enough to finish it. When the storm died down and she said she had to get back to work on thawing and repairing her garden, Adlet offered to help. He was the first man Trish allowed to do so.

Trish and Adlet never got married. Still, they were together for five years. During that time they ended up with a son called Matek. Trish remembered feeling guilty when Matek was born as she realized he looked nothing like his father. Feeling guilty because she was glad for that. Because it had come from her, she had *grown* it, and naturally, it belonged to no one else.

Adelt left when Matek was four. Trish imagined he would have left before that if the winters hadn't been so bad he wasn't able to risk the journey through Kodiak; or if he'd found another job or woman to take him in.

But before that, when he'd been younger and more naïve and full of beer, Adlet had imagined he might be able to stay in this village with this quiet, almond-eyed woman and her fantastic garden, and he'd bought her a clay pot of delphiniums in the hopes she'd agree.

Adlet wasn't much of a father anyway. He might have been if given a chance, if given a different place to do it in, but Trish was jealous and never let Matek out of her sight for a minute. Too many gardeners, after all, trod too much soil.

'Kid's gonna have problems if you don't cut the damn umbilical cord,' Adlet would say. 'Might as well still be in your friggin' belly.'

And also, Trish never wanted to leave her garden, never

wanted to leave the house, much less the village. She had never been anywhere else.

One night, when Matek was three, Trish left him home with a sitter and let Adlet take her to the bar for a few drinks. But after too many tequila shots – 'Cheers to fuckin' firewater!' he would scream – Adlet made her stand on the countertop lined with glasses and dried, sticky beer. He poured whisky around her feet and lit it with his lighter while Mac, Sila's brother, killed the lights. Trish watched the blue fire lick the wood and felt the heat on her woollen socks. She listened as they laughed and gasped and thought she would explode from holding down the screaming anger in her throat.

Trish never left Matek home again. She was so quiet sometimes people thought she was slow, but her right hook sure wasn't. Adlet sported a black eye and a swollen jaw for a week afterward. Everyone thought it was a bar fight; no one asked. And no one imagined. Because the thought of Trish being angry, much less violent was, well . . . messy. Trish and messy didn't go together.

And in a way, it was true. Trish liked to keep her borders tidy. She wasn't mean, just neat.

'Keep your garden under control,' her mother had said, 'and you'll find everything else takes care of itself. Having a garden in this godforsaken place sure is something to be proud of. Can't let it dry up once you've started, can't let it die or it's on your hands.'

In her garden, Trish often sang and smiled to herself, appraising her frosted green cabbage stalks, her dark, wide rhubarb leaves. She *was* proud of what she'd accomplished. People came to buy her vegetables, to cut her flowers. She carted her pots and baskets of plants to festivals or funerals for a moderate fee, and was pleased when complimented. She blushed easily, and mumbled shyly, but she was still pleased. She supposed it wasn't all that much in life, really, just to have a little garden in the back of her little house. And some small part inside felt that it was a great thing because she had done it all by herself. It was *hers*.

And it was enough – with Matek, that is. Because *he* was hers too.

Matek never took to gardening. She guessed he had gotten his father's thumbs after all. It was better than having his nose, or Adlet's eyes looking at her every day, wasn't it? And in truth, Trish liked having her garden to herself. Matek was another growing thing she could nurture, take care of. Another needy life in the freezing winter and pouring summer. She loved him more for being *part* of her garden than being able to take part in it.

Her grandmother taught her how to keep the herbs safe from frostbite when the temperature dropped by using plastic and fishing line. Her mother had lectured her on the necessity of keeping the plants free of weeds that would take the scanty soil, suck up the slowly-thawing nutrients. And when she learned, she grew too, seeing the stalks rise from the ground from her ministrations. *Growing* was in her blood. Having a son was an extension of that, surely – but Matek, he was unlike any seed she'd seen before. As he rose from the ground he grew less interested in her and more interested in basketball, in going to hang out in the parking lot of the grocery store with his friends, in watching television.

Still, they were close. Trish lived for her son. She didn't like to think much of Adlet, of that time in her life – it made her angry and things broke in her fisted hands before she could stop them, she hated losing control, things happening without reason, breaching the trimmed borders of her world. But it had brought Matek to her, and that was a blessing. She shared everything with him. They were friends, soul mates, she liked to think – there was nothing Matek could not tell her. As the years passed Trish became even quieter and nearly stopped talking to people altogether as she worked ceaselessly on her garden. Except for Matek, she spoke only to her plants.

But as he grew, Matek started to change. Trish remembered how he loved eating the raw rhubarb stalks after she cut and rinsed them, right off the stem. How they'd laugh as he'd pucker his mouth and squirm at the sourness, but keep right on chomping anyway. Suddenly he didn't like rhubarb anymore. Not even in her pies.

And one day he came home from school and found the glossy brochures confusingly addressed to him. The mail was never for Matek, only Trish's name appeared on the magazines, bills or the few personal letters she received. Trish briefly wondered if she would have hidden them if she'd known what they were.

'What do you want for dinner?' Trish asked.

'I dunno, whatever,' Matek said.

'How was school?'

'Okay,' he said. 'Did you look at these? The one in Idaho looks pretty cool.'

'What?' she said. 'The brochures? What are they for?'

'College, Mom. After high school? You know, my education?'

'College?' Trish said softly, standing by the stove as if she'd never heard the word before.

'Yeah, I want to go to college in the States,' he said. 'The lower forty-eight.' He waited. 'It's a dead end here, Mom. I've got to get out.' Trish nodded, silent. 'Aw, don't start crying, Mom. God, come on. You've got to stop doing this. I can't live with you for ever. You've got to get a life.'

But she *had* a life, Trish thought. Life *in* life. She had life everywhere around her – she made it. She grew it. How could he not see that? If only she could convince him, she thought. Like that lilac bush that didn't want to grow up along the wooden gate, it only needed a little encouragement, a little wire run along the stem. If only he would listen to her, she would give him such good soil; she would water him for the rest of his life.

Saturday morning Matek wasn't home and she left for the bar with the leeks for Sila.

'So, Matek and the Walker girl, is it?' Sila winked at her across the mahogany, reaching for the cardboard box Trish was holding.

'Walker girl?'

'Yeah, heard they were quite the item lately, have you met her?'

Trish shook her head. Matek told her a few days ago that the Walker girl had been missing school for almost a month. Matek had shrugged and finished his potatoes and said the rumour was she was pregnant. He had said it as if it were a joke. As if it were funny.

Trish was waiting for him when he came home.

'That girl,' she said, her eyes black. 'Did you do that to her? Did you get her pregnant?'

'Ha,' he said. 'Who told you? It wasn't a big deal.'

Trish stared at him.

Matek glowered at her. 'Mom, don't start. You don't know anything about it.' He dropped his keys on the counter and opened the fridge.

'You're going to leave for college,' Trish said evenly. 'You're just going to leave her, alone with her baby?'

Matek stood up and took a swig of milk from the carton, wiping his mouth with the back of his hand. 'Come on Mom,' he said. 'We weren't together, not really. *It wasn't a big deal*. Why should I have to stay here to take care of it? She was probably going to stay here the rest of her life anyway.'

You will be here the rest of your life, you and your fucking garden. Adlet had said that to her before he left. *You and your goddamned garden and no one else.*

'I won't stay here,' Matek said. 'I can't. Not for anyone. I'll be starting a new life, I'll be leaving everything behind.'

Everything. Trish swallowed, her head pounded. She wondered, for the first time in years, if there was aspirin in the cupboard. *I'm not going to ruin my life for you.*

'But I don't understand,' she said softly. 'How can you do this to someone you love?'

Matek stopped drinking and looked at her, the carton sweating water beads down his hand. 'What are you talking about?' he said. 'I don't love *her*.'

That night she had a dream. She was in her garden, but it wasn't her garden. Trish stood, cold in her shift and thought how silly she was not to be wearing something more, like her garden clogs or her parka, but the night was warm and she realized it was summer and that was okay. She went to her tomato plants under the plastic wrap, wound around the thin wood rising from the soil and saw an ugly black tendril leaping up like sin, poking its way through the clear

136

barrier. *Weeds.* Trish gasped and yanked the plastic off, hurriedly snatching the weed from the ground and trying to cover the tomatoes back up before the night air got to them, but just as she threw the first weed to the ground, another snaked up at the end of the row, and another. Trish felt a low growl in her throat and she ran after them but they were too much for her. She turned and suddenly they were *everywhere* – growing, slithering, spreading like green-black sickness all through her garden and she ran and ran but knew she could never get them all before they overtook her beautiful yard. *Keep your garden under control*! So she went straight for the delphiniums – she could at least save those, and somehow that seemed right in her dream, so suddenly she was there, in front of the flowerbox and she screamed because it was too late and she knew what she'd known all along, that they'd always been weeds, *weeds! – how can you do that to someone you love? –* that her garden had always been a mass of dark green festering chaos and wildness and she had only been pretending it was beautiful, only pretending she had control of this wild earth and its demonic seed and she shrank back from the rising tendrils of her own nurture and screamed and screamed as the black garden seethed and boiled around her in the frozen wilderness.

Trish woke up, feverish and cloudy. She didn't remember her dream, exactly – she hardly remembered any dreams at all. Trish didn't usually care for dreams or things of a superstitious nature. Still, she felt uneasy and it wasn't until she went downstairs and saw the kitchen in a mess, crumbs all over the floor and empty beer cans lining the sink that something finally bent in the direction it had been leaning for so long.

Suddenly she knew what Matek had become. He came into the kitchen, his shoulders bowed, his step slow. She looked at him, his skin a greenish hue from drinking the night before. He stood by the fridge, taking gulp after gulp of orange juice from the plastic jug. She watched it run in sticky yellow lines down the sides of his chin and on to his shirt. He towered over the sink, over the delphinium potted there. She looked at him, at the flower, at his gangly, selfish smile. He turned to put the orange juice back in the fridge, and the sight of his dark, slender back struck Trish like a shovel in her gut. He was starting to look like Adlet. He was *growing up* into Adlet. Pretending to be hers, fooling her all along – she finally saw the truth, the ugly, black truth. And she knew what she had to do.

He turned and looked at her.

'What?' was the last thing Matek said.

The delphinium pot was heavy and Trish's hook was fast. It only took a moment.

And then a moment to clean up the broken clay and dirt on the floor.

And then it was done.

A few months later she took more leeks to Sila at the bar.

'Haven't seen you for a while,' she said. Trish shrugged. Sila was used to her shyness. 'How's Matek liking college? Bet he's having the best time of his life,' Sila said, taking the cardboard box from Trish's hands. 'Well, it's no use being sad when they leave, you know that. He's in a better place, ain't he? It's good for him.'

Trish nodded. *It's good for him*, she thought. *For his own good*.

'You told him about that Walker girl? Had a miscarriage,

I heard. A mixed blessing, they say. She's going to head to Anchorage for college in the spring.'

Trish nodded again. 'I brought her mother some flowers,' she said softly.

'I have to say,' said Sila before Trish left. 'These are the freshest ones this year! What have you been doing?'

Trish smiled slightly, blushing. 'Weeding.'

It was hard having such a nice garden in such a cold place, Trish knew that better than anyone. But whenever someone asked her she'd shrug and give a small smile.

'Not too hard,' she'd say. 'Not too hard if you keep at it.'

The hardest thing, they'd ask?

'Weeds,' she'd say. 'It's the weeds that'll choke you if you let them alone for even a minute. I'd have no problems if it weren't for them weeds.' Trish's face would flush, her fists clench.

'Just look at the Shaw place,' she'd sniff. 'Weeds everywhere. Filthy,' Trish would say, glaring into the sunlight past her well-kept yard. 'Just don't know a good thing when they got it, them Shaws.'

LOUISE DOUGHTY

Into Each Heart

O N SUMMER evenings the light outside would fade and the garden become scoured with shadows. 'Look at the clematis,' she would say. I sat and planned every inch of her death. And now, these mild nights, I suffer no remorse. I had too much help from all those other men. Doctors and therapists and lawyers – their smiles acquit me, even now. In the deep red heart of it, we are the same.

Summer: the first-class compartment of a commuter train hurtling from the city on a Friday afternoon. The carriage is solid with sunshine – and full of men. We wear suits and ties and balance briefcases on our laps. Some of us are pretending to read but our heads are heavy and our necks unco-operative. Trickles of sweat burn in thin lines down our spines. We are uncomfortably aware of the existence of our bodies.

I think I was a little paranoid, for a while. I thought I was being stared at, everywhere I went, but particularly on this train, where I was forced to sit still for over an hour while my fellow passengers could gaze at, recognise and judge me at their leisure. I would stare straight ahead and look at none of them, my mouth set in a furious line. Or else I would languish in my seat with one foot up upon the other knee, professionally bored. It is really rather dull to be a murderer, my eyes would drawl. Why don't you look at something more interesting? You could do it. You could murder your wife or your daughter or your mistress, this very evening. I have no monopoly on misogyny. You hate them too. I can smell it.

This afternoon, for instance, this hot, choking, honest afternoon, I look at the man sitting opposite. He is large. He gazes into the window as if he is watching the passing countryside when he is, in fact, intent upon his own reflection. His fat hands are folded in his lap. He wears his face like a shroud. Who knows what that man is capable of?

Three others get off at my stop. They all have wives in absurd cars waiting for them outside the station – they hurry to them. I alone set off on foot, swinging my briefcase.

There is a track that curves down and away behind the village. In winter, it is impossibly muddy – but in summer, it is mine. I saunter with my arms outstretched to meet myself. I breathe. The sun lies in wait behind each bush and forgetfulness leaps out from every corner.

As I turn the corner at the end of the alley, I feel a soft crunch beneath my feet. Pausing and bending, I see I have crushed a snail. Killing small things always distresses me. I peer at it. It is barely recognisable. Small shreds of shell are stuck here and there in a tiny mess, a panting pile. They are all born male, snails. As they grow older, they become female – so all the young men have to creep around looking for old ladies to do the business with. In winter, snails hibernate by withdrawing into their shells, which protect them not only from predatory blackbirds but from their other great enemy: desiccation. Snails adore being moist. You will never find a snail sunbathing, stripped of its carapace, in a yellow bikini, sipping a long drink with a good old-fashioned thriller lying on the grass beside it. They can't find the sunglasses to fit.

She would sunbathe in the garden with baby oil rubbed into her cellulite and an expression of dogmatic optimism on her blotchy, pale face. Oven-ready Marsha.

The back gate to my cottage is at the end of the alley. It is rotting. The hinges are thick with rust. I lift the rope loop that holds it to the post with one finger and replace it after I have passed through. I got out of the habit of using the front entrance after I had those two journalists camping on it. If I had kept a dog I would have set it on them, but I have two fat hamsters and several tropical fish, none of which appear designed to strike terror into the heart of your average hack. It was only the tabloids that were interested, anyway – and only then because my law firm had once represented a very minor royal.

In winter, as soon as I get into the house I rush around lighting fires and drawing curtains and cooking food – but in summer, none of one's bodily desires seem that threatening. I wander to the kitchen and contemplate the bags of salad on the floor of the larder. I am fond of tomato at the moment, sliced very thinly with a sharp knife and placed on dark, unbuttered crispbread, the Swedish sort. I am on a diet.

I eat standing up, to signify that it is a practical act, meaning nothing. Sitting alone at a supper table is always poignant and best avoided if you want to keep the melancholia at bay.

The church bell-ringers begin to practice as I clear up the things from my snack. I put on my rubber gloves and wash up slowly, letting the small bubbles run over the knife. Then I stop, and stare out of the window, looking at nothing. Unwillingly, I remember.

*   *   *

In the evenings, we would sit together, she and I, wallowing in silence. The clock ticked on the mantelpiece and the light through the French windows was like sand. If we were in the mood, I would slide an Inkspot compilation into the CD player, then slump back in the armchair, watching her with eyes that translated everything.

Even then, when we were happy together, I could sense a tragedy awaiting us. How long have I known this woman? How have the years fallen upon us? The music would drift. *I don't want to set the world. On. Fi-er . . .* She had a flame in her heart.

I remember one evening. There had been a long pause. I smiled as I waited for her to ask me what I was thinking.

'What are you thinking?' I said.

'I was just thinking,' she replied, 'how terrible men are.'

'Tell me how terrible,' I said.

Outside, the air was still. There was the distant clacking of a neighbour over the hedge, deadheading roses, one by one. We slid towards a moment.

'Oh well, you know. You of all people, my dear. Where *shall* we begin? With their wanton kindness, which, as we all know, is a substitute for feeling anything. Their clumsiness? Their deceit?' I sipped my drink, nursing the glass in my hand. 'Their *self*-deceit, that is what I truly cannot stand.' She sat up slightly. She was warming to her topic. I knew she was about to talk about Susannah. The inevitability of it gave me a small pain, like indigestion. 'And if you catch them out, if you try and point it out to them, well then you are finished. That is why he left me for Susannah.'

I hated her, sitting in that chair. God how I hated her. I hated all her talk, I hated all her thoughts but most of all I hated her obsessions. I would have torn into the flesh of her

144

fat throat with my fingernails if it would have stopped her being so obsessed.

She lifted her head to smile at me. 'My poor dear. You must get so fed up with my talking about it. About him, I mean.' No, go on. Go on. 'Do you know what she was like?' She put down her glass. She let her head fall backwards again and her voice lost its emotion. She was always matter-of-fact about the things that hurt her most. She was always in the most pain when she seemed rather bored. 'She was perfect. Ten years younger than me and, oh, it showed. You can't compete with that, you know. Especially not when she's the secretary. All that servility. She wore these straight, slim skirts with little pleats. Kick pleats, I think they're called. Lovely ankles.' She lifted one of her own solid specimens and regarded it ruefully. 'I followed them one evening, not long after he left. He had told me there was no one else. They went for a walk along a cobbled street and I watched them in the rear view mirror. His hands were in the pockets of the leather jacket I gave him for Christmas.'

My attention had wandered. As she fell silent, I looked up. She gazed at me and began to cry. 'Perfect little Susannah . . . they even had babies together. What a nice life they must be leading and how . . .' She could not go on. She let her head fall and hyperventilated into the arm of the chair. The tassels on the antimacassar shivered as it slid sideways to the floor. This woman, I thought to myself, has made melodrama into an art form.

She rose from the chair and wandered over to the window. The room had grown quite cold. The lawn was shadowed. There was a little birdsong and the faraway hubbub of a mower. From the adjoining cottage, a child could be heard practising a descant recorder. The branches of the willow at the far end of the garden had reached the ground. By contrast, the room seemed suddenly quite modern. Magazines lay on the floor, beside the television.

She stood and regarded the faint reflection of herself in one of the windows. She spoke to it very softly, almost in a whisper. 'I used to dream about her, night after night. Dreams that would drive you mad. Far more often than I dreamed about him. It is terrible . . .' She bowed her head, then lifted it back up sharply. 'It is terrible to know just how ugly you are compared with another woman and just how little you are loved because of it.'

There was a silence that cut the air. I could hardly breathe. She could still affect me like that, sometimes, standing there so statuesque and defiant, daring her own reflection to love her. My God, what a woman! What a marvellous, strong, *feeling* lump of woman.

She tipped her head to one side, looking at herself.

'Am I fat?' she asked, suddenly a child.

'Yes,' I replied.

When she first started cutting herself up, it did give me cause for some concern. She started with scissors. She went for the soft flesh on the upper part of her right arm. (There was quite a bit of flesh for her to go for). She took a pair of dressmaking scissors, half-opened, and dug into herself. She did it quite slowly and with no obvious sign of pain. The skin came off in flakes and the flesh was pinkish. I examined the marks afterwards. They were parallel lines, like railway tracks, not very deep, with thin brown scabs where she had bled slightly. They took all of a week to fade.

The knives were more serious of course. No doubt she would have progressed to razor blades sooner or later, perhaps digressing with a gardening tool or two. After a while I took to throwing out as many utensils as possible to try and minimise the mess but if somebody is really determined to chop themselves up there isn't much you can do about it. There was once a type of South American Indian, so I've heard, who when captured by marauding Spaniards or Portuguese would commit suicide by biting through the arteries at the wrist with his own teeth.

I never understood it. I never wanted to.

I came across a letter the other day, when I was clearing out some of her old papers. It was written to her old schoolfriend, Alice – the only person she confided in, I think.

Dear Alice

Things have been so bad since I lost Anthony. It's back, all the dark stuff, and I don't know how to keep it at bay. We still talk on the phone, occasionally. I try and explain to him but he accuses me of melodrama. Yesterday, he told me I wouldn't be happy unless I was having a trauma of some sort. I know that is partly true but I can't tell you how deeply it hurt to hear him say it, as if all my pain is nothing.

I did it again the other evening. I knew it was going to happen hours before and I tried to stop myself. I do try. I go for walks. I read books. I play music. I ring up friends and talk quite normally about how I am and then cry as soon as I put the phone down. I sing to myself. 'I like coffee, I like tea . . .' Anything that will stop me for one minute more. Then, all at once, I become very calm. The battle is over. Slowly and with much dignity, I head for the kitchen, to the drawer where the knives are kept.

I am scared, Alice. I don't know what's going to happen.

The letter is unfinished and, of course, unsent. Alice died a year before it was written, of ovarian cancer, I believe.

And there I am again, in the sitting room, looking at her in the same chair. It is a summer evening, again. We are talking, again. We make the same shapes and the light is still like sand. Why is it always this picture I see? I would gaze at her, sometimes in hatred, sometimes in awe but always fascinated. She would gaze back. She was golden.

We were a whole person, she and I, between us. I was the part that sat on trains and earned an ordinary life. She was the hope and the despair and love and all that might endure. No one is remembered for having paid the bills. I dry the knife and plate and put them away. I close the kitchen window. I empty the bowl of washing-up water down the sink. The bubbles sink with a gurgle. A darkness is gathering in.

All at once, I am shaking. She always hated the dark. I rip off the rubber gloves. They cling to my hands like blood. I wrench at them in a panic. I throw them down and rush for the light switch. Then I run into the living room and turn on the lamp and the television. I fly around the house in a frenzy, turning on every switch, the radio in the bedroom, the hair dryer, the food mixer in the kitchen.

It doesn't stop. None of the light or noise will make it stop. *Into each heart, some tears must fall . . .*

How dare you judge me? What do you want to know. Do you want to know about the first incision, just above the left breast? I see it even now, the bloodfall with the light through the French windows like sand. I hear her scream of doubt. More? More? What about *down there*? They wanted to know, those infants with their notebooks in their hands who shouted at me through my letterbox. Prurient

148

fools. You are just as bad. You want me to feel guilty. I won't. I will push my hand against the fire, I will bite off my own fingers, I will pour burning oil over my groin but SHE IS DEAD.

Ah well. It's all blood under the bridge now.

I make the house quiet again. I go upstairs to change out of my suit. The bedroom is still lilac. It would have made sense to have it redecorated, I suppose, to something more befitting my status as a single man but I didn't want people tramping all over the place. I changed the bedclothes from all that floral stuff to some modern, asymmetric design. I threw out the scalloped vanity unit and bought a cheap, square ugly chest of drawers. I threw her maidenhair ferns out of the window, and then had to go down to the garden to clear up the mess.

And then there were the moisturisers, the lotions to stay young, lotions to stay beautiful, lotions to get beautiful in the first place. When it was all gathered together in a heap, I sat and stared at it.

What a relief to go into the bathroom now and see nothing but my humble shaving apparatus.

I sometimes wonder what Anthony would make of what happened. I wonder if he saw the newspaper reports. Probably not. He wouldn't lower himself to read a tabloid. Even if he did, he would only think he was well out of it all and blessed the day he left her for the perfectly female Susannah. Marsha thought she went mad because of his desertion but, of course, it had started long before then. There was so much else; an imperfect childhood, the usual adolescent agonies, dreams of being loved and loving in return, a barren marriage followed by an acrimonious divorce; growing old and ugly with my career thriving enough for me to buy myself this expensive little cottage in this expensive little village; using the train each morning, suits and court shoes, an honorary man and every bit as desperate.

There is no rationale, there are no reasons. There is only the terror of waking and lying there, in the darkness, knowing that the only heart beating in that room is your own.

And now I am a man.

They could never sort me out as a woman, those men on that train. I was much more of an oddity then than I am now. I always looked too old, too young, too well-off, too human to fit into any of the usual slots. I was rather too substantial to cram into a pigeonhole. They would die before they admit it but most men find me much less disturbing in trousers, even when they know my history. I know and they know I know. That is why I make them so uncomfortable. I am a cunning half-and-half; unmoved, unrepentant, and above all, amoral. Let them try and judge me now.

I am sorry. I have denied you your climax. There is no rising inferno, no torrent of blood as I reveal, laughing maniacally, by what horrid means she met her bloody end. The medical process was lengthy and dull. There were the therapists and psychiatrists – and trousers for a year before they would even look at me. Eventually, there was a feeble, testosterone beard.

Then, at last, there was the lopping off, the pruning of those things that are far more symbols of womanhood than the hidden bit. The hysterectomy was neither here nor there. They all seemed somewhat relieved, if a little bemused, when I finally plucked up the courage to reveal that I had no desire for a member. I tried to explain to one who seemed a little more perceptive than the rest.

'It is not the acquisition of the male sex that I require. It is the loss of the female. The latter is made easier by the former but it is only a means to an end. I wish to be ignored. I want to become invisible. Unfortunately, one cannot be sexless. The nearest one can come to it is to be an unattractive male. I am already unattractive. It is the second bit that requires your assistance.' The poor man stared at me in bewilderment and I felt guilty for giving him the burden of my confidence.

The part of it that really interested me was not the white coats or the diagrams or luteinising hormones but the whole psychology of it. They gave me a reading list, you know. There was one on fantasy and deviancy, as if I was concerned with sex. Oh it was all the usual stuff, women and men and mothers and fathers and how we shouldn't worry because it was all quite normal. I yawned my way through it. At the end, there was a chapter entitled, 'Women are Human Too.'

Isn't it a joke? Isn't the whole thing one almighty, breathtaking, self-consuming joke?

Can't you hear me laughing?

I draw the curtains and sit down in the chair she always sat in. I look at myself in the mirror, on the wall. I still sit here, these nights, and gaze at myself. I still see her, sometimes, brushing a wisp of hair back from her face with an impatient hand and frowning, or throwing her head back with the abandoned laugh that meant she was in trouble. She poses for me. She pouts. She accuses me – not of murder but of simple narcissism. Every now and then, she blows a little kiss.

Outside, the evening has sunk. It is May. A whole summer lies before me. A whole summer of days and days and hours to remember. I will walk down from the station five times a week in the scented air, behind the church, down the alley, through the back gate that will one day fall to pieces. I will wait while roses unfold. I will sit here and sip fruit juices and listen to the songs floating out into a garden bursting with growth. *Into each heart* . . . If I am feeling strong enough, I will indulge in a little well-earned senti-mentality. 'Summer is the time for all this,' she would say. 'Summer is the time. The hours stretch. Nothing matters except the fading light and the smell of your own skin and the clematis scrambling over the garden fence in one last desperate bid to escape. It is the time for slow plans enacted when you doze, believing dreams of idleness, stepping outside your own limiting skin and seeing yourself as if from far away, in the distance; poised, careful, and free.'

LIANNE KOLIRIN

Elvis Has Entered the Building

S OME DAYS we have this game going, usually late, when the heat of the day has passed. First, whoever is in charge makes sure nobody is around. If Manalo caught us then that would be it. We'd lose our jobs in this sweaty hangar and have nothing to do besides stay home and fight with our wives. So one of us will whistle, soft, like hardly whistling at all. The rule is that then, whatever we're doing, we stop. Everybody obeys. Me, Narciso, Oscar, Luis and the new guy who's married to Oscar's cousin Lilia. Then somebody, usually me, gets the ball. We keep it on the high shelf with the lost property. It's safe there. In the nine years I've worked here, nobody has ever come looking for anything.

Whoever called the game – the man that whistled – must then open the match. He throws the ball high above his head, swiping it down with the palm of his hand. It is up to him who he chooses to throw to and how hard he will make the other man work. Then the second man flips the ball back to someone else. The idea is to keep it in the air for as long as possible. Sometimes it lasts several minutes, other times it falls almost immediately. And the man who lets it drop is the one we call *olat*, the loser. The man who drops the ball throws it again – but this time on the carousel – with the bags going round and round, like a game of roulette. When the ball stops, the *olat* picks up the nearest piece of luggage and lays it on the floor. He has three minutes to open it, dig around and throw the bag back on to the belt. When we first started playing, the idea was to take out one thing as a kind of a souvenir, but somehow that one became two, became three, became four. If the bag is locked he cannot switch it for another. Instead he must cut it open and carry on as usual. When we're done with the contents we empty them out into a big plastic bag. We stick a label on for the passenger, explaining that the bag was 'damaged in transit'.

Today it is the new guy, Francisco, who whistles. At first he refused to play. Probably he was nervous about getting caught, but maybe now he feels more confident or maybe he wants to prove himself. I don't ask; I just try to defend my area. Problem is there's still luggage coming off the afternoon flight from Manila and almost everyone has checked in already for the return journey. There are cases that need to come off, cases that need to go back on, but rules are rules and the bags will have to wait.

Francisco passes the ball to Luis, Luis punches it to me. I use my backhand to send it flying over to Narciso. He invented our game and never lets us forget it. Like a yo-yo, he pushes and pulls the ball back and forth into the space above his head, careful not to let it hit the rusty fan rotating on the ceiling. Suddenly he strikes like a professional, sending the ball over to the door where Oscar keeps watch. From here we can see the three small aircraft sitting on the tarmac, hungry for fuel and impatient to depart. Nobody stays here for long. Either they are on their way back to Manila or straight over to the port where they will catch a boat to Boracay. I hear it takes an hour to get to the island, not that I know anybody who has been. The tourists tell us it's paradise and that we should go. Who would carry their bags on and off the flights then, I wonder.

Oscar teases us for a while, passing the ball from hand to hand. Then bouncing it up and down on his head, he walks over to the luggage trolley, picks up a couple of bags and throws them on to the belt. 'There's work to do,' he says, 'maybe we call it quits for today.' Everybody is angry and shouting at Oscar for being a coward and trying to cheat. For a moment he tries to defend himself, before shrugging his shoulders and volleying the ball back over to me. He makes me mad. He thinks he's smarter than us, because he lived in Saudi Arabia. Makes out that he's village royalty and that we should be kissing his feet. So he's been on a plane and worked abroad, so what? He talks like he was some big oil baron, but then what's he doing here, with us? My father's sister Malaya knows somebody who was in Saudi at the same time as him. This guy says Oscar was a driver for a rich sheikh and his family. Oscar used to take his wife wherever she needed to go: to pick up the children, go shopping, have her hair cut.

So now that he's started with the superior act, I decide that Oscar must lose and send the ball zooming back to the space by the door that he should be guarding. He doesn't make it. The ball, as if in slow motion, hits the doorframe, tumbles to the ground and rolls out on to the tarmac. We all run over, worried what will happen now that our game has spilled over into the outside world. Luis prods Oscar in the back and tells him to 'go get it'. Reluctantly, Oscar accepts that as loser it is his job to pick up the ball. But it's nowhere to be seen. The tarmac is clear besides the planes and a big group of passengers is making its way to the hangar. My neck grows moist with sweat and my tongue feels dry. I try not to think of where the ball might have got to. We stay by the doorway for two, three more minutes, searching through the haze of the plane fumes, half expecting the ball to roll straight back into the room. Then we hear footsteps: Manalo's for sure. So we rush to clear the cart of the remaining baggage. In marches Manalo, a cigarette filter topped with ash hanging from his grey lips.

'Finished?' he asks, not waiting for a response. 'What do I pay you for? Come on, there's a full flight for Manila that leaves in twenty-five minutes, that means a whole plane that still has to be loaded.'

Nobody answers. We shift the remaining bags on to the belt and nod.

Manalo heads back to his office. He is not quite out the door when a tiny, yapping dog comes running in from outside. It has short, curly white hair and a little red cowboy scarf tied around its neck.

The boss turns around. His face looks like the Lord Jesus has just walked up to him and requested a one-way ticket to Manila. Meanwhile, the dog slows to a stop right by Luis. It looks him straight in the eye, opens its mouth and out rolls our ball.

'Find out who owns it and get it out of here,' says Manalo as he stomps back into his office.

Luis stands there like a statue, so I walk over to the dog and pick it up. It wags its tail and licks my face, as if it has flown all this way just to see me. I stroke it a while, then walk over to my locker to see if I have anything for him to eat. There is a soft mango and a piece of chewing gum. I reach into my pocket and feel for the penknife that we use for the bags. Then I cut open the mango, kneel down and give it to the dog. Suddenly the ball comes flying overhead from Oscar's direction. The dog leaps straight up and runs like a bullet towards the ball. He follows it across the room and on to the baggage belt, which is still rotating at full speed. The ball trickles along, teasing the dog behind it. I have a bad feeling in my stomach.

'Stop it,' I shout at Oscar, at Narciso, at anyone.

They are all too busy laughing to listen. I run towards the wall myself and slam on the emergency stop button. The belt slows down and eventually stops. But it's too late as the ball rolls around the carousel and eventually finds its way on to a worn-out section. Drooling with excitement, the dog comes straight up behind the ball, tussles with it and pushes it right down through a large hole. Before we have time to pull it off, the dog – now yapping like crazy – pushes its nose, then its head, then its whole body, through the hole. The yapping stops.

We look around at each other, expressionless. I don't remember how many times Manalo has screamed at us to get the belt fixed. Now it's too late.

Out of nowhere a group of *banyaga* wearing sunglasses and floppy straw hats comes piling into the hall. From the corner of my eye I see that Oscar is laughing. The bastard.

Narciso begins to shout in Tagalog, then English, telling them that the area is restricted and not open to the public, but nobody takes any notice. There are ten, maybe twelve of them, all circling around this *acheng* in fancy clothes, with his face painted all pretty.

'But darling, one minute you were holding him and the next he was gone. Honestly, darling, you were supposed to be watching him,' cries the *acheng* in his woman's voice.

Again Narciso repeats his warning. Again there is no response. By now all the *banyaga* are crouched down on the floor, getting their expensive clothes dirty. Narciso begins to shout again. I try to calm him and instead approach the *acheng*.

'Sir, can we help?'

Two men with thick necks and arms as wide as my chest step up to my face. The *acheng* looks away – I am invisible to him. A pale woman with red hair and red shoes inter-rupts.

'His dog is missing,' she says, being careful not to speak too loud. 'I thought I saw him run in here, but we can't find him. Did any of you see him, he's about . . .'

She puts her hands out in front of her. I feel like telling her we don't get many dogs in here, so she doesn't need to be too precise with her measurements. But before I get the chance Francisco steps forward, smiling a broad, phoney smile, and says: 'Sorry Ma'am, no dog, no dog.'

'Essie, what did he say? Have they seen my petit chou-fleur?' asks the he-she.

The woman pauses. 'Apparently not,' she says.

'But why not?' he demands, stamping his feet.

I look around at the others. Narciso is picking at the rough skin on his arm, while Luis picks up the broom and chases a rogue cockroach outside.

Everyone in the group, the woman included, is now huddled around the *acheng*. They talk to him in soft, calming voices. He's a grown man. It's shameful. One of the big guys offers him a tissue, while the other fetches him a chair. He wipes a cloth over it before pushing it under his boss to sit down. I don't understand these Americans, or wherever it is these people come from.

Now the woman comes over to me, tip-tapping in her spiky red heels.

'Look,' she says. 'You seem like a reasonable guy. Just tell us where the dog is.'

She comes closer and puts her painted lips right up to my ear. She takes my hand and slips a banknote into my palm. 'For you,' she says.

I don't know what she wants, but I don't need her money and tell her so. She looks at me with angry eyes.

'Do you know who this man is?' she shouts, loud enough for everybody on the island to hear. 'Mickey Jasper is an international superstar with millions of devoted fans all over the world.'

I look over at the he-she. *A superstar*?

'He has interrupted a massive world tour to come to the Philippines and meet the poor victims of last month's devastating typhoon.'

'A typhoon? Here?' I ask.

'On the main island,' she yells. 'We've had a very long and traumatic week up there and Mickey is in desperate need of some R & R.'

'R & R?'

'Rest and relaxation! And now this! Do you know how much that dog means to him? Do you?'

She looks around the room at Narciso, Luis, Oscar and Francisco. 'If anything's happened to Elvis, there will be serious shit to deal with, believe you me. Find that dog or face the consequences.'

Mr Superstar looks up and says: 'Essie, please darling, don't talk like that. Just tell them if they find my baby we'll send them a signed picture and free tickets for my next Asian tour. And if they don't . . . well . . . I guess they'd better hire themselves a good lawyer.'

Suddenly the yapping starts up again.

'Elvis? Elvis?' shouts the *acheng*, now running around like a crazed cockerel who knows the end is near.

'Where's it coming from?' he asks the room. 'What's happened to my little Elvis? Where are you, honey bee?'

I see Luis in the corner trying hard not to laugh. Everyone else is crawling around on the floor listening out for the stupid dog. Just then I spot Oscar hovering by the carousel switch. I have to stop him . . . but it's too late as the palm of his hand swats the green button like a fly. The machine chugs into action. The barking stops, then an agonizing squeal from the dog fills the hall. It is all too much for the *banyaga*, who march around us as if war has been declared. We hear heavy footsteps in the corridor. Manalo.

With no time to think about it, I jump on to the rotating carousel. My legs are shaking and I almost lose my balance.

'What's he doing?' asks Mr Jasper.

'What the hell . . .' bellows Manalo as he walks into the room. But I don't have time to answer him or Mr Jasper. My legs move against the pull of the belt. There is a bright red case in front of me. I throw it off and find the hole underneath.

'Stop the belt,' yells Manalo.

As the carousel grinds to a halt, I lay down and lower my arm into the hole. The dog sounds close but I feel nothing down there.

'What's going on?' Manalo asks again.

'Have you got him?' says the superstar.

Ignoring them, I reach back into my pocket for the penknife. Mango juice is still dripping off it, so I wipe it on my trousers then cut a big square around the hole.

'Ramirez, I'm going to fucking kill you!' screams Manalo.

I know he means it. And if he doesn't kill me, he will certainly fire me. I keep cutting. Once the hole is big enough, I slide down into the workings of the carousel. It's dark and smells of burning rubber. On my stomach I slither along, hoping that I won't have to go too far to find Elvis. Now the squealing is louder. Somebody shines a small pocket torch into the hole. Without it, I could have missed him. But there he is, right ahead of me, curled up in a ball looking half asleep. Still on my tummy, I reach my arms out for him. A pair of watery, but grateful, eyes stare up at me. I go to stroke him, but he yelps – only then do I notice the blood dripping from his leg. Maybe he trod on a nail or a screw. Outside they are shouting, trying to get my attention, but the only important thing is to make sure the dog is all right. He wags his tail and licks my hand to reassure me, so I pull off my tee-shirt and wrap it tight around his paw. I cradle him in my arms and slither back towards the hole.

Light filters through slow at first, then brighter and brighter. The two big men reach into the opening. They grab hold of my arms and pull us both out.

'Elvis,' screeches the *acheng*, as he hurls himself at me and snatches the dog.

Manalo is in the corner shouting at Narciso and the others. Aware of the commotion, he turns around and beckons to me.

As I start to walk towards him, the woman with the red hair steps in. 'Thank you,' she says, her voice now strangely soft and feminine. 'You can't imagine how much that dog means . . .'

'Essie, I'll take over,' says Mickey Jasper. He puts his hand on my bare shoulder and looks me straight in the eye. 'Man, you have no idea how grateful I am. What can I do to repay you?'

'Nothing,' I say.

'Please,' he replies, fluttering his long eyelashes. 'Essie will take your details so we can send you tickets for my next Asian tour. I think it's Bangkok, some time next summer. That's not too far, is it?'

For him, perhaps, but for me? I don't bother to say anything – it might hurt his feelings. Instead I glance over at Manalo.

'That the boss?' he asks.

I nod and stroke the dog in his arms. 'I hope the dog's ok,' I say as I walk off.

'Wait,' says Mr Jasper, bringing the room to a standstill with a single word. Everybody stops what they are doing and looks over at him.

'I just wanted to say something.'

Manalo interrupts. 'Sir, we have a lot of flights today and these men are very busy.'

The pale woman raises her hand in the background to try and silence him. He ignores her, but stops as the two giants walk towards him.

Each of the *banyaga* looks lovingly at their boss. Me, Luis and the others avoid eye contact with ours.

'Today this man – whose name I don't even know – did a brave thing. A very brave thing. He made a difference. To me, to my friends here and, most of all, to my beloved dog. I'm not one for lengthy speeches, all I wanted to say is that Elvis and I are indebted to you, and if there's . . .'

'Ok, ok, enough . . .' blurts Manalo as he steps forward. 'Perhaps you two could continue this conversation in private. These men have work to do.'

Mr Jasper's people look ready to pounce. 'How dare he . . .' shouts somebody, as if Manalo has already left the room.

'Come,' Mr Jasper says to me, 'don't worry about him. I'll send Essie over to straighten things out.'

'He's going to fire me,' I mutter under my breath.

'No, man, no way,' says Mr Jasper. 'Everything will be cool. Trust me.'

The guys are all back around the belt, hurling the baggage on and off, trying to make up for lost time. But me, I just stand here, waiting for my fate to be sealed. Manalo walks past, the pale woman not far behind. He gives me a look that says: 'I won't forget this, Ramirez'.

Mr Jasper hands me a shirt, one of his I guess. 'Put this on,' he says. He is small for a *banyaga*, so it fits. Somebody whistles from the other side of the room. I look up and meet eyes with the others. Whistling has become a dangerous sport around here.

'Essie is sorting things out,' says Mr Jasper as he and his people float towards the main terminal building.

'Do you have your bags?' I ask.

'The guys are bringing them,' he says. 'Come through with me while I sort things out. I want to show you something.'

His dog is free and I'm pleased to have helped, but I have nothing more to say to him. All I want is to know about my job, and either to get on with it or go home. But he asks me to follow him, and for some reason I can't refuse. To me he is no more a star than my grandmother. Still, I keep walking.

As I push open the doors to the main terminal there is an eruption of bright lights and loud voices.

'Over here Mickey,' shouts one. 'Smile for the fans back home,' says another. 'Welcome to the Philippines, Mickey . . . Who's your friend?'

There are hundreds of them; Asians and westerners. They thrust their cameras, notebooks, microphones, in his face. This is why he needs the big guys.

'Shall I do something,' I ask, concerned.

'Like what?'

'Try and stop them?'

He laughs. 'Try, but it won't get you anywhere. They follow me wherever I go.'

My head throbs with this madness, but Mickey looks as if he is enjoying it. I can think of nothing worse.

'Hey, Mickey, tell us about the typhoon? What can your fans do to help the victims? And Mickey, *who is this guy?*'

All around me are bustling bodies, and I still smell ripe mango and burning rubber. I need air. We are almost at the exit, when Mr Jasper stops and turns around. He holds Elvis tightly and touches my hand. It feels like the sun is exploding in my face.

'Meet Mr Ramirez,' says the *acheng*. 'My poor Elvis got himself stuck under the baggage carousel and this man risked his own safety to get him out. He saved his life, and Elvis and I are for ever in his debt.'

Again the cameras flash like mad, but now the microphones are in front of me, practically in my mouth. I feel sick.

'What happened, Mr Ramirez? How did you save little Elvis? And what did you think when you realised who he belonged to?'

How can I tell these people the truth? That his dog got stuck because of a stupid game we were playing? That now, with all this attention, I almost wish that I had left him down there? Instead I say nothing.

Mr Jasper leans over to me. 'Don't worry,' he whispers in my ear, 'you don't have to say anything. I'll speak, and that way I can show you how grateful I really am.'

I nod. He guides me towards the door, then turns around and addresses the pack of reporters.

'Ladies and gentleman,' he says. 'Please excuse us now as Mr Ramirez is a little shy. Thank you though for being here, and perhaps now you can go back to your offices and make this man a star. Tell the world that he's a hero and that thanks to him, Elvis is alive and well and on his way to Boracay.'

KIM FLEET

Winnebago Nomad

NEV HAS an old man's toenails. Thick and yellow, they curl over the tips of his thongs. The skin on his arms has leathered deep brown, criss-crossed with fine wrinkles like spiders' threads. What does she see in him?

He's genuine Australian, my husband. He's tall and wiry and sandy-haired. His muscles are tight knots in his arms, even though he's spent all his working life in an office. He talks without opening his mouth, and squints out at you from very blue eyes. His lips are thin and peeled looking.

I've never caught on properly to this vast country, even after all these years. My face is scorched pink beneath my sunhat and my shoulders are sore. I still flap at the flies when they scurry round my nostrils and I panic when I pull hot air into my lungs.

I tried to explain it to Nev, but he just snorted and said, 'You want to go back to England? Whafor?'

'I didn't say I want to go back, just that I feel I sort of belong there.'

He shook his head at me, uncomprehending. I came to Australia when I was a teenager. Mum and Dad were looking for a new life. I can remember the life we left behind: ranks of terraced houses, the frowsy smell of the damp bathroom, sitting on the draining board in the kitchen while Mum soaped my hands and face. When our ship docked in Australia and we came onshore, I thought how empty it looked. The streets were wide and built up with houses, but it was like they were waiting for people to fill them up. The light hurt my eyes. They watered for weeks until I learned not to hang out the sheets when the sun was up and to turn my back on the glare.

I went back to Britain, years ago, and thought how cramped and dirty it looked. It made my heart ache. I was caught between the two places. I'll never see Britain again. It's funny to think of my bones crumbling in this hot sand.

Nev stamps across the shimmering tarmac and flaps his way through the coloured plastic strips hanging in the doorway. I'm sitting by the window in the roadhouse diner. Flies run over the chipped tabletop, sucking up spilt sugar.

Nev slides a bottle across to me. 'There's your pills,' he mutters.

'Maisie all full up now?'

'Don't call it Maisie. It's a van. It's a house on wheels, s'all.' He gulps at his coffee. 'Yeah, she's full. Fuel's a bloody rip-off out here.'

It's all my fault. I'd never been to the outback, but I wanted to see it, just once. And if we were going to do a big trip round Australia, we ought to do the big empty bit in the middle.

'Please, Nev,' I'd begged. 'I'd like to see it.'

The unspoken words hung in the air between us.

'Not the whole trip,' he conceded.

'Nah, just a bit of it. Up the middle to Alice, that's all.'

'And back down again.'

He rasped the side of his face and jutted his jaw, the face he pulls when he's weighing things up.

'All right,' he said, finally.

I gulp my pills down with coffee. It's cheap instant and it makes me nauseous. The woman at the roadhouse bustles over with our meals.

'Here you go, darl,' she says, placing groaning plates in front of us. 'That'll see you right.'

Homemade burgers of fresh ground beef, crisp salad, purple beetroot slithering from under the lid. Nev has an egg on the top of his. We're in the middle of nowhere. This food is a miracle, but my stomach heaves. The pills and the coffee have curdled my appetite.

'Been busy?' I ask the woman.

'Nobody all day. I tell you, I was glad when you turned in,' she says. 'You crossing the Nullarbor?'

'Nearly finished, we set off from Perth,' I say.

'Where you headed?'

'Up to Alice.'

Nev snorts. He's already tucked into his burger. He chews round and round like a camel and his Adam's apple bobs when he swallows. Egg juice slithers down his chin.

'I tell you, today's my lucky day,' says the woman, her hand resting against her hip. 'We have swallows nesting under the garage roof. They're always back by August, the same week on the dot. This year they're three weeks late, and I was frightened they weren't coming. Then this morning I saw a swallow fly in straight to the old nest. I tell you I felt so happy to see them back I almost cried. I went up and said "I thought you wasn't coming." But they're back now, and safe, and everything's all right.'

'I'm glad the swallows have come back,' I say to Nev, when she's gone.

When he doesn't answer, I push my plate across the table to him.

'Not hungry?' he asks, frowning. 'You oughta eat something.'

'You eat the burger and I'll try a bit of the salad.'

When we drive out of the roadhouse, the woman is craning her neck under the eaves, muttering away to the swallows.

'Reckon the isolation's done for her,' says Nev.

I sit up front in the campervan with Nev, and the space between us is wider than the spare seat. I imagine *her* perching there, chirping at Nev, getting in the way of the gear stick. Just in the way.

She is Maureen. She was Nev's secretary. He hasn't the imagination to pick anyone else. I wish I could write her off as a middle-aged fling, a panicking grab at youth, but she isn't. I think he loves her, truly loves her. And I think she loves him, too. I'm the one in the way. For now.

She's small and has frizzy hair and a sharp nose, and one of those high-pitched voices that goes up at the ends of sentences so you don't know if she's asking you a question or not. She was brought up on a cattle station and you'd think she'd be able to handle whatever life throws at her, but it seems she fell for Nev.

He kept her a secret for years. I mean years. It baffles me how I didn't notice what he was up to. Maybe I'd just stopped noticing Nev altogether by that time. We've been married for thirty years, enough to make anyone unobservant. But when he told me, said he wanted to leave me and start again with this Maureen, I felt real physical pain and anger like an atomic bomb waiting to go off in my chest. I screamed and cried until tears and snot dribbled down my face and into my collarbones.

I said everything I could to try and keep him. Nothing moved him. In the end, I cheated. I got cancer. I don't mean

I told him I'd got it when I hadn't, I really and truly got it, a proper big lump eating me up from the insides out. By the time I found out, there was nothing that could be done. That's when I thought of the road trip.

Lots of couples retire, cash in the superannuation, buy a motor home or caravan and set off on the big trip round Australia, seeing everything they always meant to see but were too busy to. We were just doing it a bit sooner than we expected, that's all.

Nev gave up Maureen for me. I think he felt guilty, like the cancer was a punishment for what he'd done. I helped him to feel guilty. I wanted him churned up with remorse at what he'd done. I believed he belonged with me, like the swallows belonged at the roadhouse.

It's my idea to take the Aboriginal tour. We've stopped in a small mining town. The streets are wide and dusty. Red dirt stretches to the horizon. It rubs into sweaty creases in our skin, and Nev's scalp is stained powdery orange. Gavin, our Aboriginal tour guide, picks us up in a smeary white land cruiser. The back is filled with camping gear, also stained red, and a scuffed child's tricycle. A fruit air freshener hangs from the driving mirror. He drives us out of town and back along the highway. Then a sharp right and he bumps us across rocks and down to the creek bed where he makes a fire and tells us stories. Nev is silent.

'You fellas ready for some tucker?' asks Gavin, when the sun starts to dip beneath the horizon.

Gavin tips two packets of flour into a plastic washing up bowl, then spoons in salt and milk powder. He dribbles water from a bottle, mixing the dough with his fingertips, then when it forms into a ball, he rubs it round and round the bowl with his palm.

Nev watches his hand moving. 'I'll mix me own dough,' he says.

Gavin glances up, surprised.

'Good, Nev,' I say, squirming with embarrassment. 'More damper for me and Gavin to share.'

Gavin grins at me, a flash of straight white teeth in his brown face. He cuts the damper with a crusty knife, and hands a lump to me.

'Shape it round, flatten it, and put your initials on it so's we'll know it's yours,' he says.

I form the dough, adding flour to stop it sticking. I inch it on to the wire mesh propped over the campfire. The smell of smouldering mulga logs reminds me of lapsang tea. I tell Gavin this. He laughs.

'I prefer Earl Grey,' he says.

'You what?'

'We blackfellas don't only drink the old black and gold supermarket brand,' says Gavin. He's obviously had this conversation before. I feel ashamed. 'We like a good meal and a nice glass of wine same as anybody.'

'So I've heard,' says Nev.

We watch the logs glow and shatter. Gavin takes the damper from the fire with tongs and clatters it on to a tin plate. He pulls the top off a catering size carton of butter and slides it over the sand to my feet.

'Watch him, he's hot,' he says, as he passes me my damper. The crust is hard and salty, singed with mulga smuts. Inside, the dough is soft and steaming, slick with melted butter. It rolls easily round my mouth.

'Gavin, what happens when you die?' I ask.

'For God's sake, Shirl!' cries Nev.

'I mean, what do the Aboriginal people believe?'

'Give it a rest!' Nev throws the remains of his damper into

the fire and stamps off towards the bush. He melts into the darkness and we hear his footsteps crunching over twigs and dry gum leaves.

I turn back to Gavin.

'Prickly your old fella,' he says.

'He's frightened.' I lean towards him. 'You were going to tell me.'

Gavin meets my eye. I stare back and straighten in my chair.

He bends over and draws in the sand with his fingertip.

'See, we blackfellas come in three parts,' he explains. 'We've got a body, the blood and bone, same as everyone. When you die, that goes into the dirt and turns to dust eventually.' He licks his lips and I nod for him to continue.

'Then you've got your soul. That's like a ghost, and it can hang around after you're dead, stay with your rellies and keep an eye on them. And then there's your spirit. That comes from your country, and goes back to your country when you die. In the end, it gets reborn into someone new.'

'Like reincarnation?'

'Yeah.'

'Where will your spirit go?'

He looks surprised. 'Right here, of course.' He waves his hand towards the glowing white trunks of the gum trees and the doughnuts of spinifex grass. 'Right where I came from.'

'And your ghost?'

He grins. 'It'll hang round, keep an eye on my kids and grandkids, if I get any, make sure they do the right thing.'

I laugh. 'What if you don't die here? What happens if you're not in the right place when you go?'

'Sometimes the old people can't get back home before they die,' says Gavin. 'So their spirit comes back in a willy

171

willy, a whirly wind. You don't wanna get in the way of it, that's for sure.'

I nod to show I understand.

'I better check on your old fella.' Gavin gets up and strolls over to Nev. Their voices float back to me.

'She sick your old lady?'

'Yeah.' The way Nev says it, it's like a stone dropping down his throat.

'What's up with her?'

'Cancer.'

'She got the treatment?'

'It's too late.' I hear him smack the car door. 'She did nothing, said nothing, until it was too late.'

They curse softly together, showing solidarity the way men do, the words little moths beating towards me. Fuck. Fuck, fuck, fuck mate.

'Yeah, well,' says Nev. 'No point going over it. What's done's done.'

'I'll get you back,' says Gavin. 'The old bird looks tired.'

'Cheers mate.'

Gavin drops us back at the van. He asks to look around it, seems impressed with how it all slots together.

'So yous are on walkabout?' he grins. 'Like us blackfellas?'

'That's right,' I say. 'Winnebago nomads, that's us.'

Nev sticks his hand in his pocket and pulls out a roll of notes. He peels off a red twenty and holds it out to Gavin. 'That's for taking care of us,' he says, gruffly, not meeting Gavin's eye.

'No worries, mate,' says Gavin. 'Thanks.'

Nev looks at the note held between his fingers and Gavin's. He slides another twenty off the roll and tucks it in Gavin's shirt pocket. 'You'd better treat your missus,' he says.

'That was a kind thing to do, Nev,' I say later.

'Shut up, Shirl, go to sleep.'

It rains that night, big fat drops drumming on the roof of the van. The air is heavy with the smell of rain on roasted earth. The next morning, the sky is fresh and new like a turned page. Nev says he's going into the town.

'Won't be long, Shirl,' he says, and he's off before I can speak.

I find them hidden under Nev's seat. A packet of about thirty letters from Maureen, posted to every place we've stopped on our trip. He's obviously told her the route we're taking, and she's written post restante to each place, not knowing when he'll pick it up or if it'll miss him completely. There could be orphan letters in boxes right the way round Australia.

I pull a letter out of its envelope and read it. I'm astonished. There's no hint of regret or jealousy or reproach in these letters, not after all the years she's waited for Nev. And there's nothing mushy or sentimental, either. But there's an outpouring of passion, of true unstinting love. It's an emotion I recognise and remember, and which I know has been missing from my life for a long, long time. Nev must be writing back to her because she talks about his letters. When is he writing? I haven't seen him writing. See, even after all this, I'm still unobservant.

I replace the letters and sit in the van feeling shocked, my mind whirling. I think of the swallows returning year after year to the roadhouse, and I think of Maureen waiting for Nev. And I think of Nev and me.

I remember when my mother died. She had cancer, too. I flew from Perth to Sydney to be with her. The day before she died, I came out of the hospital and saw Nev waiting outside under the hospital veranda. My heart leaped. To think he'd missed me so much, he'd taken time off work and just jumped on a plane to be with me! He'd known where to find me, and simply turned up.

It wasn't him. As I ran towards him, he turned and I saw it wasn't Nev. And I realised he'd never do anything that spontaneous anyway. Sure, he'd miss me, but it would never occur to him to jump on a plane and fly coast to coast just to be with me. Just as it never occurred to him to leave a party early and come home. If he said he was going out and he'd be home by midnight, his key scraped in the lock at five past. It never entered his head to come home at ten and surprise me.

When this dawned on me, outside the hospital, it was like I suddenly saw our love clearly, and there was a hole in the middle of it.

When I came home I told him about the man at the hospital, how I thought it was him come over as a surprise.

'Why would I do that?' he said.

'No matter,' I said.

I think a lot about this while I wait for Nev to come back from the town. When he gets back he pokes his head inside the van and finds me staring into space, thinking.

'Just off to the dunny,' he says.

He whistles as he goes. I watch him through the window. He prizes an envelope out of the back pocket of his shorts and smoothes it against his chest.

By the time he's back from the dunny I've packed and the bags are lined up outside the van.

'What's this?'

'I want you to go.'

'We haven't got to Alice, yet.'

'It doesn't matter.'

'You said you wanted to see Alice before . . .'

'Before I die,' I finish. He winces. 'Oh, give it up, Nev. This isn't what we want. You don't want to be here, now, with me.'

'I said I'd stay with you to the end, and I mean it.'

'But I don't want you, Nev.' I touch his arm. The thick blond hairs curl beneath my fingertips. 'This is the end for us. It was a long time ago, if I'm honest. Time for a new start for both of us. Just one thing.'

'What?'

'Leave me the van.'

'But you can't drive!'

'I don't need to.'

'You're not going to stay here?'

'Why not? It's as good a place as any.' I look across the red dirt to the heaps of mining spoil on the horizon. 'And you can have the van after I'm gone.'

'What am I going to do?'

'Fly back to Perth,' I say. 'Find Maureen. Surprise her.'

Nev argues, of course, but his heart isn't in it. Eventually he picks up his bags and jumps on a bus out of here. He kisses me before he goes and there are tears in his eyes, but he says nothing.

Now I sit in the shade under the awning outside the van, sipping lapsang tea and waiting for the whirly wind to take me home.

HELEN SIMPSON

Up At A Villa

T HEY WERE woken by the deep-chested bawling of an
angry baby. Wrenched from wine-dark slumber, the
four of them sat up, flustered, hair stuck with pine
needles, gulping awake with little light breaths of
concentration. They weren't supposed to be here, they
remembered that.

They could see the baby by the side of the pool, not
twenty yards away, a furious geranium in its parasol-
shaded buggy, and the large pale woman sagging above
it in her bikini. Half an hour ago they had been masters of
that pool, racing topless and tipsy round its borders, lithe
Nick chasing sinewy Tina and wrestling her, an equal
match, grunting, snakey, toppling, crashing down into
the turquoise depths together. Neither of them would let
go underwater. They came up fighting in a chlorinated
spume of diamonds. Joe, envious, had tried a timid imita-
tion grapple but Charlotte was having none of it.

'Get off!' she snorted, kind, mocking, and slipped neatly
into the pool via a dive which barely broke the water's skin.
Joe, seeing he was last as usual, gave a foolish bellow and
launched his heavy self into the air, his aimless belly slapping down disastrously like an explosion.

After that, the sun had dried them off in about a minute,
they had devoured their picnic of *pissaladière* and peaches,

downed the bottles of pink wine, and gone to doze in the shade behind the ornamental changing screen.

Now they were stuck. Their clothes and money were heaped under a bush of lavender at the other end of the pool.

'Look,' whispered Tina as a man came walking towards the baby and its mother. 'Look, they're English. He's wearing socks.'

'What's the matter with her now,' said the man, glaring at the baby.

'How should I know,' said the woman. 'I mean, she's been fed. She's got a new nappy.'

'Oh, plug her on again,' said the man crossly, and wandered off towards a cushioned sun-lounger. 'That noise goes straight through my skull.'

The woman muttered something they couldn't hear, and shrugged herself out of her bikini top. They gasped and gaped in fascination as she uncovered huge brown nipples on breasts like wheels of Camembert.

'Oh gross!' whispered Tina, drawing her lips back from her teeth in a horrified smirk.

'Be quiet,' hissed Nick as they all of them heaved with giggles and snorts and their light eyes popped, over-emphatic in faces baked to the colour of flowerpots.

They had crept into the grounds of this holiday villa, one of a dozen or more on this hillside, at slippery Nick's suggestion, since everything was *fermé le lundi* down in the town and they had no money left for entrance to hotel pools or even to beaches. Anyway they had fallen out of love over the last week with the warm soup of the Mediterranean, its filmy surface bobbing with polystyrene shards and other unsavoury orts.

'Harvey,' called the woman, sagging on the stone bench with the baby at her breast. 'Harvey, I wish you'd . . .'

'Now what is it,' said Harvey testily, making a great noise with his two-day-old copy of the *Times*.

'Some company,' she said with wounded pathos. 'That's all.'

'Company,' he sighed. 'I thought the idea was to get away from it all.'

'I thought we'd have a chance to talk on holiday,' said the woman.

'All right, all right,' said Harvey, crumpling up the *Times* and exchanging his sun-lounger for a place on the stone bench beside her. 'All right. So what do you want to talk about?'

'Us,' said the woman.

'Right,' said Harvey. 'Can I have a swim first?' And he was off, diving clumsily into the pool, losing his poise at the last moment so that he met the water like a flung cat.

'She's hideous,' whispered Tina. 'Look at that gross stomach, it's all in folds.' She glanced down superstitiously at her own body, the high breasts like halved apples, the handspan waist.

'He's quite fat too,' said Charlotte. 'Love handles, any road.'

'I'm never going to have children,' breathed Tina. 'Not in a million years.'

'Shush,' said Joe, straining forward for the next instalment. The husband was back from his swim, shaking himself like a labrador in front of the nursing mother.

' "Us",' he said humorously, wiggling a finger inside each ear, then drubbing his hair with the flats of his hands. 'Fire away then.'

She started immediately, as if she knew she only had two or three minutes of his attention, and soon the air was thick with phrases like, Once she's on solids and, You'd rather be reading the paper and, Is it because you wanted a boy? He looked dull but resigned, silent except for once protesting, What's so special about bathtime. She talked on, but like a loser, for she was failing to find the appropriate register, flailing around, pulling clichés from the branches. At some subliminal level each of the eavesdropping quartet recognised their own mother's voice in hers, and glazed over.

'You've never moaned on like this before,' marvelled Harvey at last. 'You were always so independent. Organised.'

'You think I'm a mess,' she said. 'A failure as a mother.'

'Well, you're obviously not coping,' he said. 'At home all day and you can't even keep the waste bins down.'

Nick and Tina were laughing with silent violence behind the screen, staggering against each other, tears running down their faces. Joe was mesmerised by the spectacle of lactation. As for Charlotte, she was remembering another unwitting act of voyeurism, a framed picture from a childhood camping holiday.

It had been early morning, she'd gone off on her own to the village for their breakfast baguettes, and the village had been on a hill like in a fairy-tale, full of steep little flights of steps which she was climbing for fun. The light was sweet and glittering and as she looked down over the roof tops she saw very clearly one particular open window, so near that she could have lobbed in a ten franc piece, and through the window she could see a woman dropping kisses on to a man's face and neck and chest. He was lying naked in bed and she was kissing him lovingly and gracefully, her breasts dipping down over him like silvery peonies. Charlotte had never mentioned this to anyone, keeping the picture to herself, a secret snapshot protected from outside sniggerings.

'The loss of romance,' bleated the woman, starting afresh.

'We haven't changed,' said Harvey stoutly.

'Yes we have! Of course we have!'

'Rubbish.'

'But we're supposed to change, it's all different now, the baby's got to come first.'

'I don't see why,' said Harvey. 'Mustn't let them rule your life.'

The baby had finished at last, and was asleep; the woman gingerly detached her from her body and placed her in the buggy.

'Cheer up,' said Harvey, preparing for another dip. 'Once you've lost a bit of weight, it'll all be back to normal. Romance etcetera. Get yourself in shape.'

'You don't fancy me any more,' she wailed in a last-ditch attempt to hold him.

'No, no, of course I do,' he said, eyeing the water. 'It's just a bit . . . different from before. Now that you've gone all, you know, sort of floppy.'

That did it. At the same moment as the woman unloosed a howl of grief, Nick and Tina released a semi-hysterical screech of laughter. Then – 'Run!' said Joe – and they all shot off round the opposite side of the pool, snatching up their clothes and shoes and purses at the other end. Harvey was meanwhile shouting, 'Hoi! Hoi! What the hell d'you think you're playing at!' while his wife stopped crying and his daughter started.

The four of them ran like wild deer, leaping low bushes of lavender and thyme, whooping with panicky delight, lean and light and half-naked – or, more accurately, nine-tenths naked – through the pine trees and *après-midi* dappling. They ran on winged feet, and their laughter looped the air behind them like chains of bubbles in translucent water.

High up on the swimming pool terrace the little family, frozen together for a photographic instant, watched their flight open-mouthed, like the ghosts of summers past; or, indeed, of summers yet to come.

FRANCESCA KAY

Holding the Baby

OH YOU are so pretty truth to tell, my lilyflower my wild woodrose your petal face now open up your petal mouth for me. Clean as a cat's your little tongue, that's it, wide open, open sweetheart one for Dadda one for Granma one for your Granda looking at you from up there high in heaven or down below who knows and frying, but we won't have one for Mammy sure we won't the lying godforsaken bitch no open wide one more for Dadda now. That's it. No baby don't you spit it out again it's what you need now sure it is so come on now and open up just one more little spoon, oh Jesus, what a mess come on now just one more spoon, no don't you start that up again, now hush now darling one more spoon. You'll say your Dadda's not the best of cooks and you'd be right but you can't go wrong now with an egg, a boiled egg, so come on baby one more spoon.

Go to work on an egg, I do remember, billboards on the ends of bus stops, eggs as smooth as baby's skin in blue and white striped cups. The bus stop by the dance hall, the old one derelict in Enniskillen, windows broken plastered in brown paper. Bill posters will be prosecuted, Bill Posters is innocent so he is. The Guildford five the Birmingham six the Renault fucking seven. I remember. The hens your Granma kept, the way they clucked around her heels, the way she sprayed the corn at them like drops of rain, of golden rain, their silly pecking beaks. And the warmness of their feathers when you slid your hands beneath them to steal away an egg. Warm. And soft. A new-laid egg. Chuck chuck chuck chuck chicken lay a little egg for me, my mother with her hands all full of corn and the sunshine in the morning, come on darling one more spoon. The smell of hencoops, their soft feathers.

And you were as bare as an egg that day and wet and warm and howling. Slateshine eyes, alannah, as grey and deep as mist in winter, those long winters, so long they were and I staring out of the rain-smeared window dreaming. Dreaming lights and noise and the hustle of the city, dreaming money, dreaming girls. Dreaming of your mother. Tight skirts and high high heels, white legs in high high heels, the bitch, oh come on sweetheart, just one little spoonful to fill that little belly so you'll sleep.

Sleep, well that's a joke now and not a very good one, sleep. You're a wee fat stack of nitro aren't you, safe enough if you're held upright, prone to go off if you're jolted, fast asleep I think you are but the instant that I set you down your eyes snap open like a doll's and your wee mouth too and then oh Jesus then the noise you make would wake the dead. Ah but when your eyes are shut those eyelashes of yours that grow a little every day as if a wee machine were in your eyes and winching them down slowly, tiny bit by tiny bit, the breadth of a fly's wing only or the skin inside an egg. What stops an eyelash growing or an eyebrow, I never thought to ask the question, old men have eyebrows that jut out and twist and snarl like tangleweed but they never have long eyelashes now do they? Take Mick Dorsey's eyes, why don't you, they're red-rimmed just the barest fringe of eyelash, white and stubby as a pig's. He wouldn't like that would he, Mick, to hear his eyes described so but that's what they look like yes a pig's. Narrow spiteful mean.

Mick Dorsey, not a day goes by when I don't think of him. Without Mick Dorsey where would we be, not stuck here in this rainsoaked place and our roof leaking but snug as bugs in a big bright city and I'd have your mother with me, warm and sweet and soft. You never knew a woman that had skin so soft. The first time I remember in the back of Phelan's van and her laughing, laughing saying no you're not to while she undid the buttons of her own skirt as my fingers were too frantic and not my fingers only oh sweet Jesus I thought that I was drowning there and gasping and she so warm and wet. The smell of her later on my fingers, the scent of nets still wet and only just unloaded on the quayside, dark they are then with seawater and when they dry they're flecked with salt. Did you know that fishermen seldom learn to swim? Get it over quicker that way, straight down to the rocky bottom, salt water bubbling through their lungs not bothering to fight the deep. Oh God when I think of that other man now, truffling around where I was used to, sticking his snouty stinkin self right up her in those secret places that were mine once and tasting of the sea, well I would like to kill him and kill her. A bullet between those swan-white breasts, well that would put an end to lying, right enough.

A bullet and a ballot, was that what they used to say, no it was an Armalite and a ballot box. Armalite, isn't that a pretty word now, not a pretty thing though, I'd like to stick the cold steel in her, two-faced cunting bitch. Oh sweetheart I'm so sorry did I scare you, all that shouting, naughty naughty Dadda hush. But I suppose you've got to know the story one day, but of course you've got to know the story for it's your story and it's mine as well.

Are you sitting comfortable they used to ask, a long long time ago when I was nearly your age and a story was about to be begun. Well, you're comfortable enough, alannah, as long as I keep pacing up and down. Your head damp and heavy on my shoulder and your mouth all eggy-sticky but I don't know that you'll like this story 'cos it doesn't have a happy ending and there are no fairies in it or if there are they had the sense to keep it quiet. The boyos aren't so keen on fairies although that may be out of fear of finding fairy natures in themselves. Ah but when I was a wean I used to like those stories of the wee folk in their palaces beneath the hills. They were forever trooping out under cover of the darkness and stealing the fairest human babes out of their cribs. And come the morning and their mammies would find a queer white silent waxy thing in the place where they had left their child and it would be a changeling. But don't you worry, sweetheart, I'll never let those wee folk in, I've learnt to keep my doors shut now and my ears shut too and never open up my heart.

Because that's where it all began, this story, it was because I opened up my heart. There I was for years and quiet as a clam if not as happy and minding my own business except that every now and again I'd be called on for what the boys would call my expertise. Although it doesn't really take an expert to guide a milk van through the side streets of a city right up snug and close to some barracks or a bank. And maybe a little fiddling round with an alarm clock and a scrap of wire and off you go and Bob's your uncle and best not to think what happens next but they're a load of murdering bastards aren't they, imperialist pigs and that. Although I once did see and that was just outside of Belfast, it was by mistake that I was passing, nothing at all to do with me but there was a young man on the road and his head was somewhere else. Well but that's no story for a baby, the windpipe blue and the blood so crimson oh it was a sight to stop your heart. And there was that business with the horses, rearing up the beast was, screaming, ah but that's enough now, stop. And anyway. I vowed to put an end to it, the day I met your mother. In the back of Phelan's van and her steering me into her generous sweet wetness and it was then I said I love you.

And that was the happiest time, it was. Those days and weeks and months. When she said she was expecting I was glad. Marry me, I said to her and she said oh my darling yes. And we'll get out of here, she said, this dirty drabby dreary dump and we'll go off to a big city, London maybe, or Liverpool or maybe California. They have sunshine I could be in movies I'm often told I look like Demi Moore especially now I have this bloody bump. Okay okay I said, whatever you want sweetheart, I'd have gone wherever she said I'd have leapt off the cliffs of Antrim if she'd asked. And along comes Mickey Dorsey and he laughs when I announce we're off to California, have you got stuck in time old son? he asks. Was a miner, forty-niner, no that's not the same as sixty-nine, you dirty sod.

Well, I didn't know to count the weeks, how should I, nor what Mick was meaning when he asked me had I never heard of cuckoos, well I only know of cows and chickens and in any case I couldn't give a toss. I was mad for her, I was. That look she used to give me when she was hot and ready, the time she slid her hand straight down my jeans in Jimmy's bar. Oh Jesus then I thought that I would have to come and keep a straight face too and her still laughing, talking, innocent as the first snowdrop of winter.

And then you came, all in a rush now, at the break of dawn it was, a Thursday and your mammy yelling. An ambulance with a blue light on, nee-naw nee-naw and she crying out oh holy Mary if I live through this I'll never fuck another man again. Ah well. Like every promise that she made that one was lighter than a thrush's breath. You can see it sometimes, of a winter, when a bird sings in the icy cold, a tiny breath-cloud in the air, as if you saw its song. You were like a little bird, fluttering your rib-cage, where did she get that bright red hair? my mother asked. And you were fewer than a few months old when the boys turned up, banged on the door, fingering their wads of dirty money. They were flinging it about then, they'd just done the Northern Bank, laundering money, funny way to say it, don't you think? I used to see it like a sheep dip, tenners coming out all chemical-white and then pegged out like handkerchiefs to dry. But it's not like that, oh no it's not, it's a hard and grubby trade now, do us a favour, just one last one, it's a big one, top of the range saloon we'll need, an Audi or a BMW. A VIP and whole platoons of fucking squaddies. You can take your woman, no one will suspect a woman with a wean, a real one, live and kicking, no one will look beneath its clothes.

Oh no, I said. Oh no. I've put all that behind me, I'm a father and about to be a husband, we're going to name the day soon, do it in a job lot with the christening . . . Well, we don't know that you've got a choice, the big guy said. But we'll make it worth your while so we will. And all the time your mammy listening and oh, she said, as soon as they had closed the door and gone, their money lying on the kitchen table, listen now, I have a plan. We've been dying for the bright lights, have we not? All we needed was the money, here it is. And we can double it and more if we shop the lads now, I've heard how much the Guards will pay informers, no, on second thoughts don't you do a thing. Mick Dorsey, well Mick has the connections, he'll know who to ask. We'll double-bluff the lot of them, we'll sting them good and proper, it'll be just like that film we saw, don't you worry about anything, all you have to do is nothing, not a thing at all.

Well there's one born every minute so they say but when I showed up I think even the angels must have laughed. There never was a bigger sucker saw the light of fucking day. And I suppose they're relishing the joke now, at this very moment, Mick Dorsey and your mother, wherever they are with their new names and their money, in California maybe or maybe Liverpool. What a joke it was, huh, leaving me to hold the baby, leaving me to face the music and oh God now that was a caterwauling din. Counting my blessings so I am that I am still alive and in possession of my kneecaps but it was touch-and-go, it was, forty-eight hours in a locked room and all the boys were shouting, shouting all at once and my worry the whole time was who had hold of you. Well Bill Posters was innocent so he was and lucky I was that in the end they did believe me.

But that's the only luck I've had unless I count you sweetheart whom I'm left behind to hold. And to go dancing up and down with in this room with the windows all rain-spattered and the roof leaking and nothing at all beyond it but mud and fields and far away the cold and hungry sea. And tick tick tick the clock is ticking, it's the middle of the night now and I'm thinking that you'll never go to sleep. Was my bedtime story not enough then, oh sweet Jesus, little bastard, I could shake you shake you hard. Ah but no now don't you start that up again, its okay baby, its okay really, hush for Dadda loves you and we'll go out for a walk now, shall we, count the shining stars now shall we, say good evening to the moon then shall we, hush now baby, please don't cry.

MARINA WARNER

After the Fox

The hole appeared under the thickened stem of the wisteria on the south wall of Judith's garden. It gaped too large and too deep for a vole or for a rat: Judith knew the size of their runnels, from the banks of the canal two streets away, and when she'd had the outside lavatory at the back demolished, small neat tunnel heads soon dotted the mud where the builder had trodden the old lawn. When she managed to call him back again, he kicked at the holes, and asked her for empties. Taking three wine bottles from her recycling, he dropped them into a bin liner, hammered them thoroughly till the plastic slumped like a sand bag, and then dug down into the old waste stack and stuffed it.

'They'll not make their way up through cullet,' he said.

She remembered the word: so satisfying in its finality.

But this hole was wider than a rat hole, bigger even than a cat flap: her visitor was no small burrower.

When Judith went out to look at her garden one morning, hoping to find the first cyclamen uncurling their delicate heads, she caught a panicky flash of fur and the scramble of nails on the garden wall: an animal was writhing for a foothold on the brickwork. As Judith stopped, the creature's first panic subsided and she sensed – though she could not actually see it – how the soft white fur on the inside of its pricked ears quivered to pick up her response, and hearing no reverberating anger, found its centre of gravity and levered itself on narrow, orangey haunches to propel itself with a twist and a shove up and over into her next door neighbour's.

A vixen, thought Judith, and a young one, too, far smaller than a spayed hearth cat, and scrawny. The hole must be a branch exit in a lattice of communications running under the gardens adjoining one another near her, in this part of the city where she'd lived all her adult life with Iain, until one morning in tears he said he'd always love her, but that he had to care for someone else now, as Amanda needed him more than she did: Judith was so resilient and proactive, she was a woman who could manage on her own.

Since then, Judith found that to her own way of thinking, she was now widowed: somebody dying fixes memories, defaces the present, and fills every moment with the past, ablaze. Iain not being there pressed him more brightly on her vision than Iain being there. His absence kept her mind in perpetual rewind – this *is* became this *was*, the time *now* the time *then*, this place *here* that place *there*, when he, when we did this and said that, ate this and saw that . . . the sequence, end-stopped, the frame frozen, flickered slightly in the light of her recall. The pictures screened all else, beyond now the possibility of change except for paling in patches, like colour prints leaching slowly of light.

This past mocked her as it flung at her, You didn't see it, did you. You missed the signs. You didn't know that moment was the end of it.

It pressed on, taunting: Iain is living with Amanda now, he is putting his arms around her encased bones after that crash when he was driving our car, and under the plaster cast she's growing bigger with the baby she was starting to have with him all those months. For you, the past kept on, it was the last time for this and the last time for that. But you didn't see it, did you.

She was plunging through a snowstorm, flakes spinning through darkness towards the headlights' beam and vanishing as they hit it over and over again: everything had already happened to her that was ever going to happen, and she could re-enter the sequence again at any point and it would unfold the same, a life snowbound.

So the vixen was an event, unexpected. Her apparition was a first new thing. She had never seen any kind of fox close up before, and she found herself wanting to see this one again: *Mlle Renard*, she thought. Cunning little vixen. Sharp Ears. *My* fox.

She put out apples and she made peanut butter sandwiches with stale loaf after hearing a radio programme about mange. Foxes were leaving the country, now that fields were stripped of hedges and woodland cover and poisoned with sprayings, the radio expert went on. No more hen coops and wild birds' nests – they were evolving, abandoning their traditional habitat for the spilling dustbins of the new cafés, restaurants and fast food outlets.

She felt at first a twinge of annoyance – jealousy? – to hear so many others talk about *their* foxes, but the feeling passed, to yield to a sense of belonging, just as soon after her widowhood started, she found comfort in the solitude of others like herself.

'You'll adapt,' her friend Gail said. 'You'll begin to like living alone. No more short and curlies in the plug-hole.' But Judith waved away her friend: 'I'm too old for that – my mind's not wired for change, not any more. I can't pick up Chinese as if I was four years old or start balancing a basket on my head full of stones like women building roads in

India. I can't even remember the names of flowers the way I used to, and I wish the catalogues wouldn't keep changing the botanical names – I don't know why they do this.'

Gail taught English at the local school, Judith music. But in her new widowhood, when boys and girls on secondment from Biology or Media Studies came to class, she found herself scorning their utter lack of talent for the piano, or the recorder, or, where it really stung the budding rock stars, for the guitar. Yet, before Iain went, she would throw herself into the school concert with relish, conducting till the players steamed. Before then as well she'd write without irony, '*Very* promising. *Fame* calls . . .' over and over again in her end-of-term reports, assuring her income. Now she had visions of slamming the lid down on a hapless aspiring musician when yet another mangled chord, rhythm, key, struck her newly sensitised ears. She began to think she must find something else to do, something solitary to suit her state.

After her fox came, something loosened and stirred, and as she'd always given advice from her experience of her own patch, she put a card in the local sub-post office window, offering:

'Garden Design & Maintenance
Planting Pruning Clearing Weeding Trimming
Ideas and Advice
Organic methods only.'

She gave her telephone number.

Soon afterwards, there was a message: her caller had seen the ad in the post office and needed help. 'Garden, well that might be the word . . .' he went on. The voice was melancholy, with the timbre of someone who might at one time have been able to sing. 'Could you come and give a quote? It'll have to be done from scratch.'

She rang the number; left a message.

That evening, the voice rang her:

'I was surprised by your call,' he said.

'Oh, why's that? You said . . .'

'Yes, I know, but I didn't expect a lady gardener.'

Judith wasn't sure how to respond to this; she missed her moment as conflicting feelings arose and jeered at her for failing to choose between them – scorn of that old-style gallant condescension, and – yes – a glimmer of curiosity about someone so apparently out of sync with the times and the customs of the country. Instead she told him she worked weekends only until the holidays; the appointment was made for the following Saturday.

Sean Barbett's house stood on the lane leading to the village churchyard by the river, part of the tangled waterways that connected her garden via the canal to his. On the Saturday morning when Judith cycled there along the tow path, the chestnut tree was tipped in auburn: a giant redhead standing and spreading limbs against the light. From the street, the house looked like a worker's cottage, with small deep-set windows in the tawny local stone, and, on both sides of the front door, grooves for a floodgate which was no longer there, indicating that the house was built before the canal was linked to the river to take the overspill. Which made the original building very old, thought Judith.

Her caller opened the front door and stood against the light from the garden at the back; he turned without lingering; took her straight through, down a stone-flagged passage into a kitchen at the back, an extension from the Seventies, slatted pine and roof lights and faded kilims, and slid the garden door across. She followed him out and they stood in the first scatter of leaves under a large bedraggled cherry tree. He sighed as he kicked at the mantling weeds. As he waved – shook – his hand at the knotted thickets of ground elder, nettles, and brambles, wound around with convolvulus and dying into a sodden pile of something unrecognisable left behind by a departed builder – carpet underlay? insulating lagging? – she let a small chuckle escape her.

'It makes you laugh, does it? I suppose that's good,' he said. 'It seems a hopeless task to me. Augean stables.' He paused. 'You don't do crosswords? No, of course not.'

She bridled, 'If you're worried that a woman isn't capable . . .' she stopped. 'If I'm not, I'll tell you – we might have to arrange a pick-up by the council – of the waste.' She paused, then added, 'I like digging.'

The first day, looking for tools, she found that the door to the garden shed was secured with a sturdy combination padlock. It wasn't rusty, which surprised her, as the wooden structure had grown into the damp and weedy tangle that had once been, Judith discovered as she began to work, a hedge well-planted to deliver colour each season, with crimson-stemmed cornus, winter jasmine, dark spiky juniper and red-hipped hawthorn. The threshold was trampled and the undergrowth less dense on the approach to the locked door; the small window, with its quartered pane, was curtained; she couldn't see in.

The sodden mass by the door turned out to be bedding, and crumpled wet inside the cold matted sludge that had been a duvet, lay a nightie – with rotting lace insets round the neckline. Judith kicked a fold of the bedding over it and a stab of ammonia rose from the mess and caught her by the throat till she had to clap her hand over her mouth and nose and back off fast.

When Sean Barbett came back that afternoon, he found Judith still hard at work, stretching her back as she contemplated with satisfaction the enormous pile of dead plants, living weeds, cuttings and prunings which she had cleared.

'We'll let it settle and then, you can have a bonfire night, or, as I say, we'll call the Council.' She gestured to the gunge piled by the door. 'You must have had a squatter?'

He didn't answer. He was wearing a suit and he pulled the tie loose and drew it through and rolled it in his hands, and nodded approvingly at the heap she'd made.

'Crumbs, you certainly get down to things.'

He sighed and turned, then turned back and asked her in. Leaving her boots standing outside the back door, she asked him for the combination of the padlock.

'Oh, you don't want to go in there. If you think the garden's a mess . . .'

'I thought I'd keep my stuff there – save coming through the house.' He'd shown her his garden equipment, such as it was, stowed in the broom cupboard under the stairs.

'No need.' He shook his head.

'Well, I bring most of what's necessary with me, I suppose.' It wasn't ideal, as she couldn't come on her bicycle if she had to bring large tools and couldn't leave them during the duration of the job.

'I had a wife,' he said. 'They say "partner" now, but I still think of her as my wife though we weren't official, but even so. She lived here, and it's her things in the shed, you see.'

Finding a man living on his own, Judith had him down as gay; and there was something a little gay about the way he picked so carefully around his appearance and objects, setting out tea things with an air of formality. He had been russet-haired, she could see, from the silver cockatoo crest springing from his forehead where a few freckles drifted; his hands were very white as he straightened the trivet on which he'd placed a good bone china teapot with a pattern of forget-me-nots. Looking at his fingers, she had a sudden flash: the image of these same fingers laid on her own darker flesh flickered up in her mind, weakly, hesitantly, then abated as quickly. She almost missed it, but it was something alive inside her moving, the single disturbed blade that tells the tracker something has passed this way.

The second week she was working on his garden, he returned from work and asked her, with stiff good manners, if she liked going to bed with men, and if so, would she consider going to bed with him? He did not add anything more.

He was standing near her in the garden where she was still hoeing by the light of a big lamp she'd looped over a branch. Judith told him she was out of practice; then, gesturing at her state, asked if she might use the shower first. He gave her a towel, and then, calling through the door, offered her a dressing-gown. She kept her mind on not slipping, not splashing too much, and cleansed herself with a cat's assiduity. No, she was not going to think of the possible condition of Sean's bed.

The dressing gown was silky, with embroidered panels, Chinese. When she came out he didn't say anything to her as he busied around her barely dried form. He was eager; she found herself surprised: a feeling of festivity, a flash over her limbs. He patted her and said, 'You don't seem to have forgotten how to do it.' He laughed then, and added, 'I have to say, I thought I had.'

Back in her own house, Judith went out into her own

garden and laid out food for her fox; she wanted the animal to be there, for though her sleeping with Sean surprised her, and changed the scene of her widowhood, it didn't lift the solitude.

On the radiator shelf in the hall at Sean Barbett's cottage, there drifted some small change, a few old business cards, drawing pins and paper clips and rubber bands from postman's bundles, peppermints and receipts accumulated in various chipped saucers: also, keys. Sean showed her how they were tagged to identify them: cellar, garden door, side door, front room window locks; and a slip of crumpled paper with 'garden shed' written in felt tip, and a number. She did not mean to take it in, but the digits impressed themselves as if they had spoken aloud.

She was making a rockery on the south-westerly slope at the end of the garden, where she'd collected together the old bricks and rocks she'd dug up in the rest of the plot, and as she worked, her back was to the garden shed with its mute door and small blind window with the gingham curtain tucked against it on the inside and the combination lock on the hasp across the entrance. But she felt its presence behind her; one afternoon she peeped in again through the gap where the curtain, on its wire, sagged in the centre of the window, and saw that a postcard which she felt sure wasn't there before was propped up against the pane, its picture side turned inwards, the message and the address legible on her side of the glass. It was addressed to Daisy Sulter, and came from Turkey; the caption identified the image, as 'Suleimanye mosque Very beautiful worship place'. It was old, postmarked something something 197-something, as far as she could decipher it. The message read, 'Conference boring but have played truant

and tried to find the carpet shop where we bought ours –
they all looked the same and when I asked, two merchants
at least fell on me like an old friend. Need your eye, but
shan't say wish you were here, Love, Sean PS Back before
this reaches you, probably!'

Judith swivelled the cogs on the padlock to the number
still clear in her head: the interior was in shadow, and she
took a moment or two to see what the garden shed held. It
was full of things, as Sean had warned. But whereas Judith
had envisaged a stack of tea chests, and perhaps a shelf of
rusting antifreeze and some hardened sacks of fertiliser, she
found she was looking at a tiny, neat bedroom.

The shed was a Wendy house, with a narrow, low bed,
tucked in and covered by a satin eiderdown stitched in a
floral design; one pillow set straight; a low cupboard,
doubling as a bedside table; a pair of chemist's reading
glasses lying there, next to a ewer and basin in china with
cabbage roses; on the floor, a round tatting mat, variegated,
and a pair of Wellingtons with mud on them; hanging on a
hook beside the window, the slippery satin dressing gown,
Chinese sprays of embroidery on glowing crimson panels.

Judith drew back, slipped the hinge of the lock through
the hasp with fluttering fingers, her heart pumping blood to
her temples.

'Daisy turned against me, for some reason she wouldn't
give,' Sean explained under some constraint the following
week. He resisted Judith's attempts to turn over the past.
'Perhaps she didn't know it herself.'

'But . . .' Judith wanted to object, but fell silent, not to
give away her trespassing.

'I could see I irritated her,' Sean went on, 'that my very
presence set her teeth on edge, that my touch repelled her.'
He sighed and turned towards Judith, and put a fingertip to

her shoulder above her breast. 'You are different, you see. You rather like sex. At least you seem to – with me.

'I used to think she had a lover, someone else,' he said. 'Though she wouldn't ever admit it. So one night, after a terrible time, when she rejected me and said she would never sleep with me again, I rushed out into the garden and went to sleep in the shed. After that, it became a kind of habit – injured pride, that kind of thing. Then one thing led to another – you know the rest.'

Judith didn't: except that Daisy, his first wife, had left him eight years ago, and that afterwards there had been a potter called Sylvie.

'I don't know why,' he said, again.

She tucked herself closer in to his body, thinking of the garden shed. His limbs, in which something had leaped a short while ago, now felt damp and chill.

'Then, after Daisy moved out, she sometimes came back without warning. She still had keys. Once she arrived when I was . . . Well.' He turned on to his back and lifted himself up the bed a little to laugh. 'Her appearance for all intents and purposes as if she still lived here . . . it did not please my guest, as you can imagine. But as for Daisy, she didn't turn a hair.'

'Who was that?'

'Meriel, that was her name. Pretty. Her name, I mean. She was middling good-looking. But a fine viola player. We played together in the quartet I . . .'

Now there were too many paths: the memory map was lifting into new land masses, trackless wastes, and new creatures of unknown feature and behaviour were roaming its unknown expanses.

Judith ignored Meriel for the time being. For now, she'd keep to another track:

'Where is she now? Sylvie?'

There was a pause.

'North Carolina, she has a husband there – she met him through one of her courses. She liked taking courses: Buddhism one year, caning another.' He laughed. 'Basketwork. Not the other sort. A broker husband. And children. She doesn't write. Of all the women . . . Ouch,' he broke off, as Judith pinched him, 'Well, we're not so young that we have to pretend, surely – she is the one I've most lost contact with.' He turned Judith's face with his hands to look at her, 'I'm being tactless.' It was his turn to pinch her, gently. 'Aren't you speaking to me any more?'

Every time Judith turned over something she'd retrieved from the past life Sean had lived in the house and its overgrown garden, it slipped and changed, as certain flowers under sodium street lamps turn sulphurous, an elegant pale yellow becoming dirty dishwater, and crimson blossom reddish-brown scuzz.

One afternoon, when Judith let herself into the house and walked through into the garden, Meriel was sitting at the kitchen table warming her hands on the teapot. Judith could not mistake her, in the velour hat she'd seen from one of Sean's photographs with her curling dark 'pre-Raphaelite hair' spilling out under it: she looked as she must have looked when they were together, thought Judith. An aroma of citrus and vanilla emanated from her pale skin and large, sad, ringed eyes.

She began talking about Sean to Judith without a pause, warmly, kindly, like a big sister who has learned that the youngest in the family has found a boyfriend for the first time.

'Don't you find yourself feeling sorry for him? Because he

seems so cast down by life? I know I do. Still, after all these years.

'I hope he's paying you properly. He can be very vague about that kind of thing, and when you're sleeping with him, it's sometimes a bit sensitive to ask for money.' (At this she giggled.) 'It's not his way, that, not at all. He may be hopelessly, chronically, congenitally unable to be faithful to one woman, but he would feel utterly defeated if he had to shell out for it.'

She took a sip of tea and looked up at Judith, her soft eyes moist with mischief:

'Has he peed in front of you yet? He loves that. Just a little boy at heart.' She laughed. 'With a big whoosh. Oh, intimacy with Sean is a game, just a game.' She pushed a cup towards Judith and began pouring.

'And has he swivelled you round yet when you're having sex? So you're upside down on top of him? He thinks that's awfully clever.'

Making her way downstairs, she saw the door to the side of the main bedroom was ajar. It led to a kind of glory hole, where Sean tossed things he didn't want to throw away. She pushed it open and looked inside. Flung on the chair was a skirt, a good, shapely skirt, made of some kind of soft wool in a deep maroon brown. She was magnetised by it, plucked it from its place; it was warm to the touch, and wafted a scent of something alive as she lifted it. The skirt filled as she held it up to the shape of the hips and limbs of the wearer.

Judith began writing Sean a letter. It went through several drafts, many of them blotted with tears and thrown away; these were all far more impassioned, even hysterical than the one she sent:

Dear Sean,

I am afraid that my eyes were bigger than my stomach, as the saying goes, and you were right, the work on your garden has proved too much for me in the end. I've made a good start, I hope you'll agree, and I hope you'll be able to take it from there to your satisfaction.

I wish you well,
Judith

PS Do keep putting down egg shells to deter slugs and snails, and if it's dry, please remember to water, as drought will kill the new plantings very quickly.

On the phone the evening he had her note, Sean sounded shocked; he did not understand what had happened.

'There hasn't been anybody here', he said.

When he came round to find her at her house later that evening, he appeared so genuinely baffled, she told him.

'Even if Meriel really did come to see me, I didn't see her,' he said. 'Besides, I didn't invite her, and I know nothing about it. Also, it's quite possible for her to come round and for us to have a drink together, surely?'

She wanted to cry out, from the most boring depths of her hurt, 'But how did she get in?'

'And I promise you,' Sean went on. 'You have nothing to fear from her. She has shown no sign of returning, now, or at any time. Nor has Daisy, nor has Sylvie. And not for want of my trying to persuade them.'

Judith flinched.

'Not now, silly. *Then.*' He paused. 'You have a past, too. You have . . . Iain.' He looked out of her window on to the garden, which lay in darkness now. 'There are always others. We're old enough to have lives around us. We've travelled old tracks, gone to earth more than once.' He turned back to her. 'Don't be angry about this.'

The groundwork on Sean's garden was done, and so they moved into a different phase, for there was no obvious pretext for their meetings. She had to own up to herself that she wanted to be with him, that he wasn't casually profiting from her employment. Sometimes, she even talked to him unguardedly: unaccustomed new feelings sprang at her, like the flash of a pair of night-seeing eyes from the canal bank when she cycled to and from Sean's, or the brush of her vixen, bushier now from all that peanut butter laid out by Judith (and by neighbours too, no doubt) and flaring for an instant in the long evening light as she swivelled into her earth.

When autumn closed in towards winter, Judith bought some mastic and squeezed out a fillet round the window-panes of the garden shed to improve the insulation; she found a plant rack and some shelving and installed them, regardless of occupants. There she began potting and layering, bringing on slips and cuttings for the planting she was planning for the spring. She had in mind clustered shrubs and ground cover in contrasting shapes and colours, aromatics for the edges of the path to the shed so that the leaves would release their perfume as she and Sean went past looking for a new bud here, picking out a stray shoot there. She imagined it as it would be: her head was moving with pictures from the future, and the past was jostling for attention at the back of the class, sticking up its hands and messing about, calling out 'Miss, gotta go to the toilet.' She was quelling it with her crossest look, but it was disruptive, it wasn't going to cooperate.

In the shed one morning, a woolly hat appeared, a rich rust colour, with a furry trim, tossed into a basket next to a good make of secateurs. Judith did not remember seeing either of them before, any more than Sylvie's skirt (it was Sylvie's, Sean confirmed). She plucked the hat out of the basket and pulled it on, then checked herself in the pane, which against the dark glossy foliage of the new camellia she'd planted beside the shed, acted as a mirror. It suited her: she looked as if she was up to something, something not to be anticipated or understood before it occurred. Still wearing the hat, she went back through the house, and up the stairs, and into the glory hole. She pulled the skirt from its new position on a hanger, and still in her gardening T-shirt, jeans and socks, stepped into its soft folds. She went into the bedroom and made a tentative turn in front of the mirror. She liked the effect: there was something raffish about this outfit. It turned her into a kind of stranger to herself, a new visitor in her own life, and the encounter was not unpleasant.

Back in the shed, she went on thumbing in seedlings, then, using the secateurs, cut up into knubby lengths a good section of iris root she'd sliced from a friend's choked clump. As the night drew in, she began to set it carefully into the flower bed on what would be the sunniest patch of the garden in the spring.

When Sean came back from work later, she met him, and, delighted with her outlandishness, insisted on keeping on every bit of clothing when they went to bed so that the skirt's fullness was spread all about the bed under them both, rucked and twisted and right messed up. She found she enjoyed the sex better than the time before or the time before that. Such satisfaction it delivered, to watch Sylvie hovering there, on the landing outside the bedroom door, in her jacket and tights and boots, but without her skirt.

When a nightdress turned up with the Chinese dressing gown again on the back of the bathroom door a few days later, Judith took a shrewd look at the fabric and the workmanship and appreciated the fine blue lawn with cotton lace trim.

She was humming the theme from one of her favourite pieces of Bach while she let fall her clothes on to the bathroom floor and put on the nightie. When she walked down the stairs and saw Daisy sitting reading in a chair by the fire in the sitting room, she started, of course. But this time, Judith hardly quailed; almost without pause, she turned back on her heel and went upstairs, and standing in the bedroom, pushed her fists into her eyes until the snowflakes needling into her burst into flowers of colour and light, and then she turned on the electric blanket in anticipation, waiting for Sean to come back so that they could do what they liked to do and have sex before supper.

About the Authors

TREZZA AZZOPARDI was born in Cardiff. Her first novel, *The Hiding Place*, was published in 2000. It won the Geoffrey Faber Memorial Prize and was shortlisted for both the Booker Prize and the James Tait Black Memorial Prize. Her second novel, *Remember Me*, was published in 2004. She lives in Norwich with her partner Stephen Foster.

VALE BENSON has had short stories published in various magazines and anthologies, including *Mslexia* and the Macallan/Scotland on Sunday *Shorts 4* (published by Polygon). She has also had work broadcast on Radio 4 and Irish national radio and read on the Eildon Tree/Scottish Arts Council CD, *Eildon Leaves*. In addition to her own writing she has designed and run successful autobiographical writing courses for Scottish Borders Council. She lives in Edinburgh and is currently working on a faction novel.

JESSICA BOWMAN is a graduate student completing the MA Writing Programme at Middlesex University. She graduated with Honours from the University of Puget Sound, in Washington State, with a Bachelor's in Creative Writing and was voted Creative Writing Student of the Year in 2002. She won Puget Sound's Freshman Writing Award in 1999 for her short story, 'Rattlesnake Kings', and published four poems in the University arts magazine, *Cross-currents*, from 1998 to 2002. She is currently working on a novel for her Master's thesis, and hopes to have other short stories in publication in the States later this spring.

CARYS DAVIES won second prize in the inaugural Orange/*Harpers & Queen* Short Story Competition and was longlisted for the Fish International Short Story Prize 2005, and was runner-up in the 2005 Bridport International Short Story Prize. Her stories have also appeared in the *London Magazine* and in the US in *Press, G. W. Review, MacGuffin, New Letters* and *Kestrel*. She is married with four children and lives in Lancaster.

LOUISE DOUGHTY is the author of four novels, most recently *Fires in the Dark*, about a Roma family living in Central Europe during the Second World War which was published to widespread critical acclaim in 2003. Her fifth novel, *Stone Cradle*, will be published in May 2006. She also writes plays for radio and has worked widely as a journalist and broadcaster.

HELEN DUNMORE is a novelist, poet and short-story writer. She won the inaugural Orange Prize for Fiction for *A Spell of Winter*, the McKitterick Prize for *Zennor in Darkness*, and the Poetry Society's Alice Hunt Bartlett Award for *The Sea Skater*. Her most recent novel is *Mourning Ruby* (2003) and her latest collection of poems is *Out of the Blue* (2001). She is a Fellow of the Royal Society of Literature.

KIM FLEET has an MA and PhD in Anthropology from the University of St Andrews. She lived in Australia for a number of years, working with Aboriginal people in the field of native title land rights. Her experiences in Australia informed her short story 'Winnebago Nomad'. An avid scribbler of stories since she was a child, she has had some stories published and has been placed in a number of short-story competitions. She is currently seeking publication for far too many novel manuscripts, and is working on a new novel about land rights and black–white relations in Australia. She also has a proper job as a researcher in Norwich.

ALEXANDRA FOX is a mother and grandmother from a Northamptonshire village who still regrets that she never went to university. She unexpectedly started writing short stories in 2004 and has now won more than fifteen first prizes in literary competitions as well as numerous placings and publications, print and web, including a Supplementary Prize in Bridport 2005 and an out-of-the-blue commission from Virgin Atlantic to write for their in-flight magazine. Her uncompromising story 'Bonsai' was nominated for Best of Web. Lexie writes with Alex Keegan's online Boot Camp and finds (as do her family) that writing has taken over her life.

BRIDGET FRASER writes about things which matter to her and as her way of exploring emotional landscapes. To date, she has published one slim (very) volume of poetry, *And the grass still grows* . . . and has had several poems accepted for anthologies. Following a law degree and a career as a journalist, Bridget now promotes contemporary art exhibitions. She is currently completing her first novel, set in Herefordshire, and a collection of short stories drawn from the time she spends in West Bengal where she also has an art gallery.

TARA GOULD. After completing an MA in creative writing, Tara won the Jerwood/Arvon Award for young writers. She has since worked as a creative writing tutor for CCE at Sussex University and a script reader for a film production and financing company. Last year she completed a collection of short stories and is currently embarking on her first novel. She is also involved in a number of community-based writing projects. Tara was commissioned to write for a drama documentary broadcast on Radio 4 last year. She lives with her partner and two children in Brighton.

SALLY HINCHCLIFFE graduated from Birkbeck with an MA in Creative Writing where she was one of the team who set up and edited the inaugural issue of the *Mechanics' Institute Review*. Her story 'Gerald Says' was broadcast in January 2005 on Radio 4, and she has read another story, 'The Witching Hour', at the Tales of the Decongested. She is currently writing her first novel, *The Year List*. She works at Kew Gardens and lives in south London.

ROMI JONES grew up in a family where literary gaps were filled with Irish traditions of storytelling and reinventing the truth. After decades of scribblings, she is now working on a novel, a collection of short stories and has completed a Creative Writing MA at Newcastle University. In 2004 she was runner-up in the Biscuit Publishing annual competition. Romi has worked with community groups and charities for over twenty years. She lives on the north Northumberland coast.

FRANCESCA KAY was born in London, spent her childhood in South-East Asia and in India (where her mother is from), went to a convent boarding school in Surrey and read English at Oxford. Her subsequent career as a civil servant was cut short when she got married and went to live in Jamaica. From there she moved to Washington DC, Germany and Ireland, before coming back to Oxford where she now lives with her three children. She has had part-time jobs, such as caring for small children with special needs, but in the past few years has tried to give as much time as she can to writing.

ANNIE KIRBY was born in 1971 and lives in Dorset. She has an MA in Creative Writing from the University of East Anglia and is currently writing a novel called *Blood Hands Moon Snow*. In 2004 her short story, 'Revelations of Divine Love', was published in the anthology *Bracket: A New Generation in Fiction*, and in the same year 'Orchid, Cherry-Blossom' was broadcast on Radio 4 as part of their 'Ones to Watch' series focusing on new writers.

LIANNE KOLIRIN was born in Israel in 1972. She is a freelance journalist, working mainly at the *Daily Express*. She recently finished an MA writing course at Middlesex University, where she produced a collection of short stories entitled *Short Stay Parking*. Lianne lives in north London with her husband and their young family.

KATE PULLINGER'S books include the novels *Weird Sister*, *The Last Time I Saw Jane* and *Where Does Kissing End?* and the short-story collections, *My Life as a Girl in a Men's Prison* and *Tiny Lies*. Her most recent novel, *A Little Stranger*, will be published in 2006. Kate also writes for film and radio as well as for digital media; you can find her latest multi-media piece, *The Breathing Wall*, at www.katepullinger.com. She is currently the Royal Literary Fund's Virtual Fellow and teaches on the Creative Writing MA at the University of East Anglia.

HELEN SIMPSON won the *Sunday Times* Young Writer of the Year Award and a Somerset Maugham Award for her first collection of short stories, *Four Bare Legs in a Bed and Other Stories* (1990). She was chosen as one of Granta magazine's Twenty Best of Young British Novelists in 1993. *Dear George* was published in 1995 and *Hey Yeah Right Get A Life* (2000) – stories about motherhood – won the Hawthornden Prize. Her fourth collection, *Constitutional*, was published in 2005.

LYNNE TRUSS is an author, journalist and broadcaster, famous for her bestseller on punctuation, *Eats, Shoots and Leaves* (2003). She has published three novels, a book of columns and has written numerous comedies, plays and series for BBC radio. She was sports columnist for *The Times* for four years. She lives in Brighton.

MARINA WARNER is a writer of fiction, history and criticism. Her most recent books include *The Leto Bundle*, a novel, and *Murderers I Have Known*, a collection of stories. Her Clarendon lectures at Oxford were published as *Fantastic Metamorphoses, Other Worlds* in 2002 and her essays have been collected in *Signs and Wonders* (2004). *Phantasmagoria: Spirit Metaphors and Modern Media* will appear in 2006.

A NOTE ON THE TYPE

The text of this book is set in Linotype Sabon, named after the type founder, Jacques Sabon. It was designed by Jan Tschichold and jointly developed by Linotype, Monotype and Stempel, in response to a need for a typeface to be available in identical form for mechanical hot metal composition and hand composition using foundry type.

Tschichold based his design for Sabon roman on a fount engraved by Garamond, and Sabon italic on a fount by Granjon. It was first used in 1966 and has proved an enduring modern classic.